"I don't care what you think!"

How could Javier be so *cool and composed* when she was *all over the place*? Except, of course, she knew how. Because Sophie was just so much more affected by him than he was by her and she could see all her pride and self-respect disappearing down the drain if she didn't get a grip on the situation *right now*.

She cleared her throat and stared at him and through him. "I... We have to work alongside one another for a while...and...this was just an unfortunate blip. I would appreciate it if you never mention it again. We can both pretend that it never happened, because it will never happen again."

Javier lowered his eyes and tilted his head to one side as if seriously considering what she had just said.

So many challenges in that single sentence. Did she really and truly believe that she could close the book now that page one had been turned?

He'd tasted her and one small taste wasn't going to do. Not for him and not for her. Whatever her backstory, they both needed to sate themselves in one another. And sooner or later it *would* happen...

Cathy Williams can remember reading Harlequin books as a teenager, and now that she is writing them, she remains an avid fan. For her, there is nothing like creating romantic stories and engaging plots, and each and every book is a new adventure. Cathy lives in London, and her three daughters—Charlotte, Olivia and Emma—have always been, and continue to be, the greatest inspirations in her life.

Books by Cathy Williams

Harlequin Presents

Seduced into Her Boss's Service
The Wedding Night Debt
A Pawn in the Playboy's Game
At Her Boss's Pleasure
The Real Romero
The Uncompromising Italian
The Argentinian's Demand
Secrets of a Ruthless Tycoon
Enthralled by Moretti
His Temporary Mistress
A Deal with Di Capua
The Secret Casella Baby
The Notorious Gabriel Diaz

The Italian Titans

Wearing the De Angelis Ring
The Surprise De Angelis Baby

One Night With Consequences

Bound by the Billionaire's Baby

Visit the Author Profile page at Harlequin.com for more titles.

Cathy Williams

A VIRGIN FOR VASQUEZ

HARLEQUIN PRESENTS®

Recycling programs
for this product may
not exist in your area.

ISBN-13: 978-0-373-13449-6

A Virgin for Vasquez

First North American Publication 2016

Copyright © 2016 by Cathy Williams

Printed in U.S.A.

www.Harlequin.com

A VIRGIN FOR VASQUEZ

CHAPTER ONE

JAVIER VASQUEZ LOOKED around his office with uncon-
cealed satisfaction.

Back in London after seven years spent in New York
and didn't fate move in mysterious ways…?

From his enviable vantage point behind the floor-to-
ceiling panes of reinforced rock-solid glass, he gazed
down to the busy city streets in miniature. Little taxis
and little cars ferrying toy-sized people to whatever
important or irrelevant destinations were calling them.

And for him…?

A slow, curling smile, utterly devoid of humour,
curved his beautiful mouth.

For him, the past had come calling and that, he knew,
accounted for the soaring sense of satisfaction now filling him because, as far as offices went, this one, spectacular though it was, was no more or less spectacular
than the offices he had left behind in Manhattan. There,
too, he had looked down on busy streets, barely notic-
ing the tide of people that daily flowed through those
streets like a pulsing, breathing river.

Increasingly, he had become cocooned in an ivory

tower, the undisputed master of all he surveyed. He was thirty-three years old. You didn't get to rule the concrete jungle by taking your eye off the ball. No; you kept focused, you eliminated obstacles and in that steady, onward and upward march, time passed by until now...

He glanced at his watch.

Twelve storeys down, in the vast, plush reception area, Oliver Griffin-Watt would already have been waiting for half an hour.

Did Javier feel a twinge of guilt about that?

Not a bit of it.

He wanted to savour this moment because he felt as though it had been a long time coming.

And yet, had he thought about events that had happened all those years ago? He'd left England for America and his life had become consumed in the business of making money, of putting to good use the education his parents had scrimped and saved to put him through, and in the process burying a fleeting past with a woman he needed to consign to the history books.

The only child of devoted parents who had lived in a poor *barrio* in the outskirts of Madrid, Javier had spent his childhood with the driving motto drummed into him that to get out, he had to succeed and to succeed, he had to have an education. And he'd had to get out.

His parents had worked hard, his father as a taxi driver, his mother as a cleaner, and the glass ceiling had always been low for them. They'd managed, but only just. No fancy holidays, no flat-screen tellies for the house, no chichi restaurants with fawning waiters. They'd made do with cheap and cheerful and every single penny had been put into savings for the time when they would send their precociously bright son to university in England. They had known all too well the temptations waiting for anyone stupid enough to go off the rails. They had friends whose sons had taken up with gangs, who had died from drug overdoses, who had lost the plot and ended up as dropouts kicked around on street corners.

That was not going to be the fate of their son.

If, as a teenager, Javier had ever resented the tight controls placed on him, he had said nothing.

He had been able to see for himself, from a very young age, just what financial hardship entailed and how limiting it could be. He had seen how some of his wilder friends, who had made a career out of playing truant, had ended up in the gutter. By the time he had hit eighteen, he had made his plans and nothing was going to derail them: a year or two out, working to add to the money his parents had saved, then university, where he would succeed because he was bright— brighter than anyone he knew. Then a high-paying job. No starting at the ground level and making his way up slowly, but a job with a knockout financial package. Why not? He knew his assets and he had had no intention of selling himself short.

He wasn't just clever.

Lots of people were clever. He was also sharp. Sharp in a streetwise sort of way. He possessed the astuteness of someone who knew how to make deals and how to spot where they could be made. He knew how to play rough and how to intimidate. Those were skills that were ingrained rather than learnt and, whilst they had no place in a civilised world, the world of big business wasn't always civilised; it was handy having those priceless skills tucked up his sleeve.

He'd been destined to make it big and, from the age of ten, he had had no doubt that he would get there.

He'd worked hard, had honed his ferocious intelligence to the point where no one could outsmart him and had sailed through university, resisting the temptation to leave without his Master's. A Master's in engineering opened a lot more doors than an ordinary degree and he wanted to have the full range of open doors to choose from.

And that was when he had met Sophie Griffin-Watt. The only unexpected flaw in his carefully conceived life plan.

She had been an undergraduate, in her first excitable year, and he had been on the last leg of his Master's, already considering his options, wondering which one to take, which one would work best for him when he left university in a little under four months' time.

He hadn't meant to go out at all but his two housemates, usually as focused as he was, had wanted to celebrate a birthday and he'd agreed to hit the local pub with them.

He'd seen her the second he'd walked in. Young, impossibly pretty, laughing, head flung back with a drink in one hand. She'd been wearing a pair of faded jeans, a tiny cropped vest and a denim jacket that was as faded as the jeans.

And he'd stared.

He never stared. From the age of thirteen, he'd never had to chase any girl. His looks were something he'd always taken for granted. Girls stared. They chased. They flung themselves in his path and waited for him to notice them.

The guys he'd shared his flat with had ribbed him about the ease with which he could snap his fingers and have any girl he wanted but, in actual fact, getting girls was not Javier's driving ambition. They had their part to play. He was a red-blooded male with an extremely healthy libido—and, as such, he was more than happy to take what was always on offer—but his focus, the thing that drove him, had always been his remorseless ambition.

Girls had always been secondary conquests.

Everything seemed to change on the night he had walked into that bar.

Yes, he'd stared, and he'd kept on staring, and she hadn't glanced once at him, even though the gaggle of girls she was with had been giggling pointing at him and whispering.

For the first time in his life, he had become the pursuer. He had made the first move.

She was much younger than the women he usually dated. He was a man on the move, a man looking ahead to bigger things—he'd had no use for young, vulnerable girls with romantic dreams and fantasies about settling down. He'd gone out with a couple of girls in his years at university but, generally speaking, he had dated and slept with slightly older women—women who weren't going to become clingy and start asking for the sort of commitment he wasn't about to give them. Women who were experienced enough to understand his rules and abide by them.

Sophie Griffin-Watt had been all the things he'd had no interest in and he'd fallen for her hook, line and sinker.

Had part of that driving obsession for her been the fact that he'd actually had to try? That he'd had to play the old-fashioned courting game?

That she'd made him wait and, in the end, had not slept with him?

She'd kept him hanging on and he'd allowed it. He'd been happy to wait. The man who played by his own rules and waited for no one had been happy to wait because he'd seen a future for them together.

He'd been a fool and he'd paid the price.

But that was seven years ago and now...

He strolled back to his chair, leant forward and buzzed his secretary to have Oliver Griffin-Watt shown up to his office.

The wheel, he mused, relaxing back, had turned full circle. He'd never considered himself the sort of guy who would ever be interested in extracting revenge but the opportunity to even the scales had come knocking on his door and who was he to refuse it entry...?

* * *

'You did what?'

Sophie looked at her twin brother with a mixture of clammy panic and absolute horror.

She had to sit down. If she didn't sit down, her wobbly legs would collapse under her. She could feel a headache coming on and she rubbed her temples in little circular movements with shaky fingers.

Once upon a time, she'd been able to see all the signs of neglect in the huge family house, but over the past few years she'd become accustomed to the semi-decrepit sadness of the home in which she and her brother had spent their entire lives. She barely noticed the wear and tear now.

'What else would you have suggested I do?' There was complaint in his voice as he looked at his sister.

'Anything but that, Ollie,' Sophie whispered, stricken.

'So you went out with the guy for ten minutes years ago! I admit it was a long shot, going to see him, but I figured we had nothing to lose. It felt like fate that he's only been back in the country for a couple of months, I just happen to pick up someone's newspaper on the tube and, lo and behold, who's staring out at me from the financial pages…? It's not even as though I'm in London all that much! Pure chance. And, hell, we need all the help we can get!'

He gestured broadly to the four walls of the kitchen which, on a cold winter's night, with the stove burning and the lights dimmed, could be mistaken for a cosy and functioning space but which, as was the case now, was shorn of any homely warmth in the glaring, bright light of a summer's day.

'I mean…' His voice rose, morphing from complaint to indignation. 'Look at this place, Soph! It needs so much work that there's no way we can begin to cover the cost. It's eating every penny we have and you heard what the estate agents have all said. It needs too much work and it's in the wrong price bracket to be an easy sell. It's been on the market for two and a half years! We're never going to get rid of it, unless we can do a patch-up job, and we're never going to do a patch-up job unless the company starts paying its way!'

'And you thought that running to…to…' She could barely let his name pass her lips.

Javier Vasquez.

Even after all these years the memory of him still clung to her, as pernicious as ivy, curling round and round in her head, refusing to go away.

He had come into her life with the savage, mesmerising intensity of a force-nine gale and had blown all her neat, tidy assumptions about her future to smithereens.

When she pictured him in her head, she saw him as he was then, more man than boy, a towering, lean, commanding figure who could render a room silent the minute he walked in.

He had had presence.

Even before she'd fallen under his spell, before she'd even spoken one word to him, she'd known that he was going to be dangerous. Her little clutch of well-bred, upper-middle-class friends had kept sneaking glances at him when he'd entered that pub all those years ago, giggling, tittering and trying hard to get his attention. After the first glance, she, on the other hand, had kept her eyes firmly averted. But she hadn't been able to miss the banging of her heart against her ribcage or the way her skin had broken out in clammy, nervous perspiration.

When he'd sauntered across to her, ignoring her friends, and had begun talking to her, she'd almost fainted.

He'd been doing his Master's in engineering and he was the cleverest guy she'd ever met in her life. He was so good-looking that he'd taken her breath away.

He'd been also just the sort of boy her parents would have disapproved of. Exotic, foreign and most of all… unashamedly broke.

His fantastic self-assurance—the hint of unleashed power that sat on his shoulders like an invisible cloak— had attracted and scared her at the same time. At eighteen, she had had limited experience of the opposite sex and, in his company, that limited experience had felt like no experience at all. Roger, whom she had left behind and who had been still clinging to her, even though she had broken off their very tepid relationship, had scarcely counted even though he had been only a couple of years younger than Javier.

She'd felt like a gauche little girl next to him. A gauche little girl with one foot poised over an unknown abyss, ready to step out of the comfort zone that had been her privileged, sheltered life.

Private school, skiing holidays, piano lessons and

horse riding on Saturday mornings had not prepared her for anyone remotely like Javier Vasquez.

He wasn't going to be good for her but she had been as helpless as a kitten in the face of his lazy but targeted pursuit.

'We could do something,' he had murmured early on when he had cornered her in that pub, in the sort of seductive voice that had literally made her go weak at the knees. 'I don't have much money but trust me when I tell you that I can show you the best time of your life without a penny to my name…'

She'd always mixed with people just like her: pampered girls and spoilt boys who had never had to think hard about how much having a good night out might cost. She'd drifted into seeing Roger, who'd been part of that set and whom she'd known for ever.

Why? It was something she'd never questioned. Oliver had taken it all for granted but, looking back, she had always felt guilty at the ease with which she had always been encouraged to take what she wanted, whatever the cost.

Her father had enjoyed showing off his beautiful twins and had showered them with presents from the very second they had been born.

She was his princess, and if occasionally she'd felt uneasy at the way he'd dismissed people who were socially inferior to him, she had pushed aside the uneasy feeling because, whatever his faults, her father had adored her. She'd been a daddy's girl.

And she'd known, from the second Javier Vasquez had turned his sexy eyes to her, that she was playing with fire, that her father would have had a coronary had he only known...

But play with fire she had.

Falling deeper and deeper for him, resisting the driving desire to sleep with him because...

Because she'd been a shameless romantic and because there had been a part of her that had wondered whether a man like Javier Vasquez would have ditched her as soon as he'd got her between the sheets.

But he hadn't forced her hand and that, in itself, had fuelled her feelings towards him, honed and fine-tuned them to the point where she had felt truly alive only when she'd been in his company.

It was always going to end in tears, except had she known just how horribly it would all turn out...

'I didn't think the guy would actually agree to see me,' Oliver confessed, sliding his eyes over to her flushed, distressed face before hurriedly looking away. 'Like I said, it was a long shot. I actually didn't even think he'd remember who I was... It wasn't as though I'd met him more than a couple of times...'

Because, although they were twins, Oliver had gone to a completely different university. Whilst she had been at Cambridge, studying Classics with the hope of becoming a lecturer in due course, he had been on the other side of the Atlantic, going to parties and only intermittently hearing about what was happening in her life. He'd left at sixteen, fortunate enough to get a sports scholarship to study at a high school, and had dropped out of her life aside from when he'd returned full of beans during the holidays.

Even when the whole thing had crashed and burned a mere few months after it had started, he had only really heard the edited version of events. Anyway, he had been uninterested, because life in California had been far too absorbing and Oliver, as Sophie had always known, had a very limited capacity when it came to empathising with other people's problems.

Now she wondered whether she should have sat him down when he'd eventually returned to the UK and given him all the miserable details of what had happened.

But by then it had been far too late.

She'd had an engagement ring on her finger and Javier had no longer been on the scene. Roger Scott had been the one walking up the aisle.

It didn't bear thinking about.

'So you saw him…' *What did he look like? What did he sound like? Did he still have that sexy, sexy smile that could make a person's toes curl?* So much had happened over the years, so much had killed her youthful dreams about love and happiness, but she could still remember, couldn't she?

She didn't want to think any of those things, but she did.

'Didn't even hesitate,' Oliver said proudly, as though he'd accomplished something remarkable. 'I thought I'd have to concoct all sorts of stories to get to see the great man but, in fact, he agreed to see me as soon as he found out who I was…'

I'll bet, Sophie thought.

'Soph, you should see his office. It's incredible. The guy's worth millions. More—billions. Can't believe he was broke when you met him at university. You should have stuck with him, sis, instead of marrying that creep.'

'Let's not go there, Ollie.' As always, Sophie's brain shut down at the mention of her late husband's name. He had his place in a box in her head, firmly locked away. Talking about him was not only pointless but it tore open scabs to reveal wounds still fresh enough to bleed.

Roger, she told herself, had been a learning curve and one should always be grateful for learning curves, however horrible they might have been. She'd been young, innocent and optimistic once upon a time, and if she was battle-hardened now, immune to girlish day-dreams of love, then that was all to the good because it meant that she could never again be hurt by anyone or anything.

She stood up and gazed out of the patio doors to the unkempt back garden which rolled into untidy fields, before spinning round, arms folded, to gaze at her brother. 'I'd ask you what he said…' her voice was brisk and unemotional '…but there wouldn't be any point because I don't want to have anything to do with him. He's…my past and you shouldn't have gone there without my permission.'

'It's all well and good for you to get sanctimonious, Soph, but we need money, he has lots of it and he has a connection with you.'

'He has no connection with me!' Her voice was high and fierce.

Of course he had no connection with her. Not un-less you called *hatred* a connection, because he would hate her. After what had happened, after what she had done to him.

Suddenly exhausted, she sank into one of the kitchen chairs and dropped her head in her hands for a few moments, just wanting to block everything out. The past, her memories, the present, their problems. *Everything.*

'He says he'll think about helping.'

'What?' Appalled, she stared at him.

'He seemed very sympathetic when I explained the situation.'

'*Sympathetic.*' Sophie laughed shortly. The last thing Javier Vasquez would be was sympathetic. As though it had happened yesterday, she remembered how he had looked when she had told him that she was breaking up with him, that it was over between them, that he wasn't the man for her after all. She remembered the coldness in his eyes as the shutters had dropped down. She remembered the way he had sounded when he had told her, his voice flat and hard, that if he ever clapped eyes on her again it would be too soon… That if their paths were ever to cross again she should remember that he would never forget and he would never forgive…

She shivered and licked her lips, resisting the urge to sneak a glance over her shoulder just to make sure that he wasn't looming behind her like an avenging angel.

'What exactly did you tell him, Ollie?'

'The truth.' He looked at his twin defensively. 'I told him that the company hit the buffers and we're struggling to make ends meet, what with all the money that ex of yours blew on stupid ventures that crashed and burned. He bankrupted the company and took us all down with him.'

'Dad allowed him to make those investments, Oliver.'

'Dad…' His voice softened. 'Dad wasn't in the right place to stop him, sis. We both know that. Roger got away with everything because Dad was sick and getting sicker, even if we didn't know it at the time, even if we were all thinking that Mum was the one we had to worry about.'

Tears instantly sprang to Sophie's eyes. Whatever had happened, she still found it hard to blame either of her parents for the course her life had eventually taken.

Predictably, when her parents had found out about Javier, they had been horrified. They had point-blank refused to meet him at all. As far as they were concerned, he could have stepped straight out of a leper colony.

Their appalled disapproval would have been bad enough but, in the wake of their discovery, far more than Sophie had ever expected had come to the surface, rising to the top like scum to smother the comfortable, predictable lifestyle she had always taken for granted.

Financial troubles. The company had failed to move with the times. The procedures employed by the company were cumbersome and time-consuming but the financial investment required to bring everything up to date was too costly. The bank had been sympathetic over the years as things had deteriorated but their patience was wearing thin. They wanted their money returned to them.

Her father, whom she had adored, had actually buried his head in his hands and cried.

At the back of her mind, Sophie had stifled a spurt of anger at the unfairness of being the one lumbered with these confidences while her brother had continued to enjoy himself on the other side of the world in cheerful, ignorant bliss. But then Oliver had never been as serious as her, had never really been quite as responsible.

She had always been her father's 'right-hand man'.

Both her parents had told her that some foreigner blown in from foreign shores, without a penny to his name, wasn't going to do. They were dealing with enough stress, enough financial problems, without her *taking up with someone who will end up being a sponge, because you know what these foreigners can be like... The man probably figures he's onto a good thing...*

Roger was eager to join the company and he had inherited a great deal of money when his dear parents had passed away. And hadn't they been dating? Wasn't he already like a member of the family?

Sophie had been dumbstruck as her life had been sorted out for her.

Yes, she had known Roger for ever. Yes, he was a perfectly okay guy and, sure, they had gone out for five minutes. But *he wasn't the one for her* and she'd broken it off even before Javier had appeared on the scene!

But her father had cried and she'd never seen her dad in tears before.

She had been so confused, torn between the surging power of young love and a debt of duty towards her parents.

Surely they wouldn't expect her to quit university when she was only in her first year and loving it?

But no. She'd been able to stay on, although they hoped that she would take over the company alongside Roger, who would be brought on board should they cement a union he had already intimated he was keen on.

He was three years older than her and had experience of working for a company. He would sink money into the company, take his place on the board of directors...

And she, Sophie had read between the lines, would have to fulfil her obligations and walk up the aisle with him.

She hadn't been able to credit what she had been hearing, but seeing her distraught parents, seeing their shame at having to let her down and destroy her illusions, had spoken so much more loudly and had said so much more than mere words could convey.

Had Roger even known about any of these plans? Was that why he'd been refusing to call it quits between them even though they'd been seeing one another for only less than eight months before she had left for university? Had he already been looking to a future that involved her parents' company?

She had called him, arranged to see him, and had been aghast when he had told her that he knew all about her parents' situation and was keen to do the right thing. He was in love with her, always had been...

With no one in whom to confide, Sophie had returned to university in a state of utter confusion—and Javier had been there. She had mentioned nothing but she had allowed herself to be absorbed by him. With him, she could forget everything.

Swept along on a heady tide of falling in love, the panic she had felt at what was happening on the home front had been dulled. Her parents had not mentioned the situation again and she had uneasily shoved it to the back of her mind.

No news was good news. Wasn't that what everyone said?

She surfaced from the past to find a drink in front of her and she pushed it aside.

'I've got another appointment to see the bank tomorrow,' she said. 'And we can change estate agents.'

'For the fourth time?' Oliver gave a bark of laughter and downed his drink in one gulp. 'Face it, Soph. The way things are going, we'll be in debt for the rest of our lives if we're not careful. The company is losing money. The house will never sell. The bank will take it off our hands to repay our overdraft and we'll both be left homeless. It's not even as though we have alternative accommodation to return to. We don't. You bailed university to get married and moved into the family pile with Roger. I may have stayed on to get my diploma, but by the time I got back here everything had changed and we were both in it together. Both here, both trying to make the company work…' His voice had acquired the bitter, plaintive edge Sophie had come to recognise.

She knew how this would go. He would drink away his sorrows and wake up the following morning in a blurry, sedated haze where all the problems were dulled just enough for him to get through the day.

He was, she had been forced to accept, a weak man not made for facing the sort of situation they were now facing.

And she hated that she couldn't do more for him.

He was drinking too much and she could see the train coming off the tracks if things didn't change.

Did she want that? Wasn't there too much already on her conscience?

She shut down that train of thought, shut down the deluge of unhappy memories and tried hard to focus on the few bright things in her life.

She had her health.

They might be struggling like mad trying not to drown but at least Mum was okay, nicely sorted in a cottage in Cornwall, far from the woes now afflicting herself and her brother.

It might have been a rash expenditure given the dire financial circumstances, but when Gordon Griffin-Watt had tragically died, after a brief but intense period of absolute misery and suffering, it had seemed imperative to try to help Evelyn, their mother, who was herself frail and barely able to cope. Sophie had taken every spare penny she could from the scant profits of the company and sunk it all into a cottage in Cornwall, where Evelyn's sister lived.

It had been worth it. Her mother's contentment was the brightest thing on the horizon, and if she was ignorant about the extent of the troubles afflicting her twins, then that was for her own good. Her health would never be able to stand the stress of knowing the truth: that they stood to lose everything. One of the sweetest things Gordon Griffin-Watt had done had been to allay her fears about their financial situation while dealing with his own disastrous health problems, which he had refused to tell his wife about. She had had two strokes already and he wasn't going to send her to her grave with a third one.

'Vasquez is willing to listen to what we have to say.'

'Javier won't do a thing to help us. Trust me, Ollie.' *But he would have a merry time gloating at how the mighty had fallen, that was for sure.*

'How do you know?' her brother fired back, pouring himself another drink and glaring, challenging her to give him her little lecture about staying off the booze.

'Because I just do.'

'That's where you're wrong, sis.'

'What do you mean? What are you talking about? And should you…be having a second drink when it's not yet four in the afternoon?'

'I'll stop drinking when I'm not worrying 24/7 about whether I'll have a roof over my head next week or whether I'll be begging in the streets for loose change.' He drank, refilled his glass defiantly, and Sophie stifled a sigh of despair.

'So just tell me what Javier had to say,' she said flatly. 'Because I need to go and prepare information to take with me to the bank tomorrow.'

'He wants to see you.'

'He…*what*?'

'He says he will consider helping us but he wants to discuss it with you. I thought it was pretty decent of him, actually…'

A wave of nausea rushed through her. For the first time ever, she felt that at the unseemly hour of four in the afternoon she could do with a stiff drink.

'That won't be happening.'

'You'd rather see us both living under a bridge in London with newspapers as blankets,' Oliver said sharply, 'rather than have a twenty-minute conversation with some old flame?'

'Don't be stupid. We won't end up *living under a bridge with newspapers as blankets…*'

'It's a bloody short drop from the top to the bottom, Soph. Can take about ten minutes. We're more than halfway there.'

'I'm seeing the bank tomorrow about a loan to broaden our computer systems…'

'Good luck with that! They'll say no and we both know that. And what do you think is going to happen to that allowance we give Mum every month? Who do you think is going to support her in her old age if we go under?'

'Stop!' Never one to dodge reality, Sophie just wanted to blank it all out now. But she couldn't. The weight of their future rested on her shoulders, but Oliver…

How could he?

Because he didn't know, she thought with numb defeat. What he saw was an ex who now had money and might be willing to lend them some at a reasonable rate for old times' sake. To give them a loan because they had nowhere else to turn.

She could hardly blame him, could she?

'I told him that you'd be at his office tomorrow at

six.' He extracted a crumpled piece of paper from his pocket and pushed it across the table to her.

When Sophie flattened it out, she saw that on it was a scribbled address and a mobile number. Just looking at those two links with the past she had fought to leave behind made her heart hammer inside her.

'I can't make you go and see the man, Sophie.' Oliver stood up, the bottle of whisky in one hand and his empty glass in the other. There was defeat in his eyes and it pierced her heart because he wasn't strong enough to take any of this. He needed looking after as much as their mother did. 'But if you decide to go with the bank, when they've already knocked us back in the past and when they're making noises about taking the house from us, then on your head be it. If you decide to go, he'll be waiting for you at his office.'

Alone in the kitchen, Sophie sighed and rested back in the chair, eyes closed, mind in turmoil.

She had been left without a choice. Her brother would never forgive her if she walked away from Javier and the bank ended up chucking her out. And her brother was right; the small profits the company was making were all being eaten up and it wouldn't be long before the house was devouring far more than the company could provide. It was falling down. Who in their right mind wanted to buy a country mansion that was falling down, in the middle of nowhere, when the property market was so desperate? And they couldn't afford to sell it for a song because it had been remortgaged...

Maybe he'd forgotten how things had ended, she thought uneasily.

Maybe he'd changed, mellowed. Maybe, just maybe, he really would offer them a loan at a competitive rate because of the brief past they'd shared.

Maybe he'd overlook how disastrous that brief past had ended…

At any rate, she had no choice, none at all. She would simply have to find out…

CHAPTER TWO

SOPHIE STARED UP at the statement building across the frenzied, busy street, a soaring tower of glass and chrome.

She'd never had any driving desire to live in London and the crowds of people frantically weaving past her was a timely reminder of how ill-suited she was to the fierce thrust of city life.

But neither had she ever foreseen that she would be condemned to life in the tiny village where she had grown up, out in rugged Yorkshire territory. Her parents had adored living there; they'd had friends in the village and scattered in the big country piles sitting in their individual acres of land.

She had nothing of the sort.

Having gone to boarding school from the age of thirteen, her friends were largely based in the south of England.

She lived in a collapsing mansion, with no friends at hand with whom she could share her daily woes, and that in itself reminded her why she was here.

To see Javier.

To try to pursue a loan so that she could get out of her situation.

So that she and her brother could begin to have something of a life free from daily worry.

She had to try to free herself from the terror nibbling away at the edges of her resolute intentions and look at the bigger picture.

This wasn't just some silly social visit. This was...*a business meeting*.

She licked her lips now, frozen to the spot while the crowds of people continued to swerve around her, most of them glaring impatiently. There was no time in London to dawdle, not when everyone was living life in the fast lane.

Business meeting. She rather liked that analysis because it allowed her to blank out the horrifying personal aspect to this visit.

She tried to wipe out the alarming total recall she had of his face and superimpose it with the far more manageable features of their bank manager: bland, plump, semi-balding...

Maybe he had become bland, plump and semi-balding, she thought hopefully as she reluctantly propelled herself forward, joining the throng of people clustered on the pavement, waiting for the little man in the box to turn green.

She had dressed carefully.

In fact, she wore what she had planned to wear to visit the bank manager: black knee-length skirt, crisp white blouse—which was fine in cool Yorkshire, but horribly uncomfortable now in sticky London—and flat black pumps.

She had tied her hair back and twisted it into a sensible chignon at the nape of her neck.

Her make-up was discreet and background: a touch of mascara, some pale lip gloss and the very sheerest application of blusher.

She wasn't here to try to make an impression. She was here because she'd been pushed and hounded into a corner and now had to deal with the unfortunate situation in a brisk and businesslike manner.

There was no point travelling down memory lane because that would shatter the fragile veneer of self-confidence she knew she would need for this...*meeting*.

Another word she decided she rather liked.

And, at the end of the day, Oliver was happy. For the first time in ages, his eyes had lit up and she'd felt something of that twin bond they had shared when they'd been young but which seemed to have gone into hiding as their worries had begun piling up.

She took a deep breath and was carried by the crowd to the other side of the road as the lights changed. And then she was there, right in front of the building. Entering when most of the people were heading in the opposite direction because, of course, it was home time and the stampede to enjoy what remained of the warm weather that day was in full swing.

She pushed her way through the opaque glass doors and was disgorged into the most amazing foyer she had ever seen in her entire life.

Javier, naturally, didn't *own* the building, but his

company occupied four floors at the very top and it was dawning on her that when Oliver had labelled him a 'billionaire' he hadn't been exaggerating.

You would have to have some serious money at your disposal to afford to rent a place like this, and being able to afford to rent four floors would require *very* serious money.

When had all that happened?

She'd reflected on that the evening before and now, walking woodenly towards the marble counter, which at six in the evening was only partially staffed, she reflected on it again.

When she'd known him, he hadn't had a bean. Lots of ambition, but at that point in time the ambition had not begun to be translated into money.

He had worked most evenings at the local gym in the town centre for extra cash, training people on the punching bags. If you hadn't known him to be a first-class student with a brain most people would have given their right arm for, you might have mistaken him for a fighter.

He hadn't talked much about his background but she had known that his parents were not well off, and when she had watched him in the gym, muscled, sweaty and focused, she had wondered whether he hadn't done his fair share of fighting on the streets of Madrid.

From that place, he had gone to...*this*: the most expensive office block in the country, probably in Europe... A man shielded from the public by a bank of employees paid to protect the rich from nuisance visits...

Who would have thought?

Maybe if she had followed his progress over the years, she might have been braced for all of this, but, for her, the years had disappeared in a whirlpool of stress and unhappiness.

She tilted her jaw at a combative angle and squashed the wave of maudlin self-pity threatening to wash away her resolve.

Yes, she was told, after one of the women behind the marble counter had scrolled down a list on the computer in front of her, Mr Vasquez was expecting her.

He would buzz when he was ready for her to go up.

In the meantime…she was pointed to a clutch of dove-grey sofas at the side.

Sophie wondered how long she would have to wait. Oliver had admitted that he had had to wait for absolutely ages before Javier had deigned to see him and she settled in for the long haul. So she was surprised when, five minutes later, she was beckoned over and told that she could take the private lift to the eighteenth floor.

'Usually someone would escort you up,' the blonde woman told her with a trace of curiosity and malicious envy in her voice. 'I suppose you must know Mr Vasquez…?'

'Sort of,' Sophie mumbled as the elevator doors pinged open and she stepped into a wonder of glass that reflected her neat, pristine, sensible image back at her in a mosaic of tiny, refracted detail.

And then, thankfully, the doors smoothly and quietly shut and she was whizzing upwards, heart in her mouth, feeling as though she was about to step into the lion's den…

* * *

She was on her way up.

Javier had never been prone to nerves, but he would now confess to a certain tightening in his chest at the prospect of seeing her in a matter of minutes.

Of course he had known, from the second her brother had entered his offices with a begging bowl in his hand, that he would see Sophie once again.

As surely as night followed day, when it came to money, pride was the first thing to be sacrificed.

And they needed money. Badly. In fact, far more badly than Oliver had intimated. As soon as he had left, Javier had called up the company records for the family firm and discovered that it was in the process of free fall. Give it six months and it would crash-land and splinter into a thousand fragments.

He smiled slowly and pushed his chair back. He linked his fingers loosely together and toyed with the pleasurable thought of how he would play this meeting.

He knew what he wanted, naturally.

That had come as a bit of a surprise because he had truly thought that he had put that unfortunate slice of his past behind him, but apparently he hadn't.

Because the very second Oliver had opened his mouth to launch into his plaintive, begging speech, Javier had known what he wanted and how he would get it.

He wanted *her*.

She was the only unfinished business in his life and he hadn't realised how much that had preyed on his mind until now, until the opportunity to finish that business had been presented to him on a silver platter.

He'd never slept with her.

She'd strung him along for a bit of fun, maybe because she'd liked having those tittering, upper-class friends of hers oohing and aahing with envy because she'd managed to attract the attention of the good-looking bad boy.

Didn't they say that about rich, spoilt girls—that they were always drawn to a bit of rough because it gave them an illicit thrill?

Naturally, they would never *marry* the bit of rough. That would be unthinkable!

Javier's lips thinned as he recalled the narrative of their brief relationship.

He remembered the way she had played with him, teasing him with a beguiling mixture of innocence and guileless, sensual temptation. She had let him touch but he hadn't been able to relish the full meal. He'd been confined to starters when he had wanted to devour all courses, including dessert.

He'd reached the point of wanting to ask her to marry him. He'd been offered the New York posting and he'd wanted her by his side. He'd hinted, saying a bit, dancing around the subject, but strangely for him had been too awkward to put all his cards on the table. Yet she must have suspected that a marriage proposal was on the cards.

Just thinking about it now, his insane stupidity, made him clench his teeth together with barely suppressed anger.

She was the only woman who had got to him and the only one who had escaped him.

He forced himself to relax, to breathe slowly, to release the cold bitterness that had very quickly risen to the surface now that he knew that he would be seeing her in a matter of minutes.

The woman who had…yes…*hurt him*.

The woman who had used him as a bit of fun, making sure that she didn't get involved, saving herself for one of those posh, upper-class idiots who formed part of her tight little circle.

He was immune to being hurt now because he was older and more experienced. His life was rigidly controlled. He knew what he wanted and he got what he wanted, and what he wanted was the sort of financial security that would be immune to the winds of change. It was all that mattered and the only thing that mattered.

Women were a necessary outlet and he enjoyed them but they didn't interrupt the focus of his unwavering ambition. They were like satellites bobbing around the main planet.

Had he only had this level of control within his grasp when he'd met Sophie all those years ago, he might not have fallen for her, but there was no point in crying over spilt milk. The past could not be altered.

Which wasn't to say that there couldn't be retribution…

He *sensed* her even before he was aware of the hesitant knock on the door.

He had given his secretary the afternoon off. He'd been in meetings all afternoon, had returned to his offices only an hour previously, and something in him wanted to see Sophie without the presence of his secretary around.

He had brought Eva back with him from New York. A widow in her sixties, originally from the UK anyway with all her family living here, she had been only too glad to accompany him back to London. She could be trusted not to gossip, but even so…

Seeing Sophie after all this time felt curiously *intimate*.

Which was something of a joke because *intimacy* implied some level of romance, of two people actually wanting to be in one another's company…

Hardly the case here.

Although, if truth be told, he was almost *looking forward* to seeing the woman again, whilst she…

He settled back in his leather chair and mused that *he* was probably the last person in the world *she* wanted to see.

But needs must…

'Enter.'

The deep, controlled tenor of that familiar voice chilled Sophie to the bone. She took a deep breath and nervously turned the handle before pushing open the door to the splendid office which, in her peripheral vision, was as dauntingly sophisticated as she had mentally predicted.

She had hoped that the years might have wrought changes in him, maybe even that her memory might have played tricks on her. She had prayed that he was no longer the hard-edged, proud, *dangerous* guy she had once known but, instead, a mellow man with room in his heart for forgiveness.

She'd been an idiot.

He was as *dangerous* as she remembered. More

so. She stared and kept on staring at the familiar yet unfamiliar angles of his sinfully beautiful face. He'd always been incredibly good-looking, staggeringly exotic with finely chiselled features and lazy dark eyes with the longest eyelashes she had ever seen on a guy.

He was as sinfully good-looking as he had been then, but now there was a cool self-possession about him that spoke of the tough road he had walked to get to the very top. His dark, dark eyes were watchful and inscrutable as she finally dragged her mesmerised gaze away from him and made her way forward with the grace and suppleness of a broken puppet.

And then, when she reached the chair in front of his desk, it dawned on her that she hadn't been invited to sit down, so she remained hovering with one hand on the back of the chair, waiting in tense, electric silence…

'Why don't you sit down, Sophie?'

He looked at her, enjoying the hectic colour in her cheeks, enjoying the fact that she was standing on shaky legs in front of him, in the role of supplicant.

And he was enjoying a hell of a lot more than that, he freely admitted to himself…

She was even more beautiful than the image he had stored in his mind carefully, as he had discovered, wrapped in tissue paper, waiting for the day when the tissue paper would be removed.

He couldn't see how long or short her hair was but it was still the vibrant tangle of colour it had been when he had first met her. Chestnut interweaved with copper with strands of strawberry blonde threaded through in a colourful display of natural highlights.

And she hadn't put on an ounce over the years. Indeed, she looked slimmer than ever. Gaunt, even, with smudges of strain showing under her violet eyes.

Financial stress would do that to a person, he thought, especially a person who had been brought up to expect the finest things in life.

But for all that she was as beautiful as he remembered, with that elusive quality of hesitancy that had first attracted him to her. She looked like a model, leggy, rangy and startlingly pretty, but she lacked the hard edges of someone with model looks and that was a powerful source of attraction. She had always seemed to be ever so slightly puzzled when guys spun round to stare at her.

Complete act, he now realised. Just one of the many things about her that had roped him in, one of the many things that had been fake.

'So…' he drawled, relaxing back in his chair. 'Where to begin? Such a long time since we last saw one another…'

Sophie was fast realising that there was going to be no loan. He had requested an audience with her *because he could*, because he had *known* that she would be unable to refuse. He had asked to see her so that he could send her away with a flea in her ear over how he thought he had been treated by her the last time they had been together.

She was sitting here in front of him simply because revenge was a dish best served cold.

She cleared her throat, back ramrod-straight, hands clutching the bag on her lap, a leftover designer relic back from the good old days when money, apparently, had been no object.

'My brother informs me that you might be amenable to providing us with a loan.' She didn't want to go down memory lane and, since this was a business meeting, why not cut to the chase? He wasn't going to lend them the money anyway, so what was the point of prolonging the agony?

Though there was some rebellious part of her that was compelled to steal glances at the man who had once held her heart captive in his hand.

He was still so beautiful. A wave of memories washed over her and she seemed to see, in front of her, the guy who could make her laugh, who could make her tingle all over whenever he rested his eyes on her; the guy who had lusted after her and had pursued her with the sort of intent and passion she had never experienced in her life before.

She blinked; the image was gone and she was back in the present, cringing as he continued to assess her with utterly cool detachment.

'Tut-tut-tut, Sophie. Don't tell me that you seriously expected to walk into my office and find yourself presented with a loan arrangement all ready and waiting for you to sign, before disappearing back to… remind where it is…the wilds of Yorkshire?' He shook his head with rueful incredulity, as though chastising her for being a complete moron. 'I think we should at least relax and chat a bit before we begin discussing… *money*…'

Sophie wondered whether this meant that he would

actually agree to lend them the money they so desperately needed.

'I would offer you coffee or tea, but my secretary has gone for the day. I can, of course...' He levered himself out of the chair and Sophie noted the length and muscularity of his body.

He had been lean and menacing years ago, with the sort of physical strength that can only be thinly hidden behind clothes. He was just as menacing now, more so because he now wielded power, and a great deal of it.

She watched as he made his way over to a bar, which she now noticed at the far side of his office, in a separate, airy room which overlooked the streets below on two sides.

It was an obscenely luxurious office suite. All that was missing was a bed.

Heat stung her cheeks and she licked her lips nervously. For all she knew, he was married with a couple of kids, even though he didn't look it. He certainly would have a woman tucked away somewhere.

'Have a drink with me, Sophie...'

'I'd rather not.'

'Why not?'

'Because...' Her voice trailed off and she noted that he had ignored her completely and was now strolling towards her with a glass of wine in his hand.

'Because...what?' Instead of returning to his chair, he perched on the edge of his desk and looked down at her with his head tilted to one side.

'Why don't you just lay into me and get it over and done with?' she muttered, taking the drink from him and nursing the glass. She stared up at him defiantly, her violet eyes clashing with his unreadable, dark-as-night ones. 'I knew I shouldn't have come here.'

'Lay into you?' Javier queried smoothly. He shrugged. 'Things happen and relationships bite the dust. We were young. It's no big deal.'

'Yes,' Sophie agreed uneasily.

'So your brother tells me that you are now a widow...'

'Roger died in an accident three years ago.'

'Tragic. You must have been heartbroken.'

'It's always tragic when someone is snatched away in the prime of their life.' She ignored the sarcasm in his voice; she certainly wasn't going to pretend to play the part of heartbroken widow when her marriage had been a sham from beginning to end. 'And perhaps you don't know but my father is also no longer with us. I'm not sure if Ollie told you, but he suffered a brain tumour towards the end. So life, you see, has been very challenging, for me and my brother, but I'm sure you must have guessed that the minute he showed up here.' She lowered her eyes and then nervously sipped some of the wine before resting the glass on the desk.

She wanted to ask whether it was okay to do that or whether he should get a coaster or something.

But then, really rich people never worried about silly little things like wine glass ring-marks on their expensive wooden desks, did they?

'You have my sympathies.' Less sincere condolences had seldom been spoken. 'And your mother?'

'She lives in Cornwall now. We...we bought her a little cottage there so that she could be far from... Well,

her health has been poor and the sea air does her good…
And you?'

'What about me?' Javier frowned, eased himself off
the desk and returned to where he had been sitting.

'Have you married? Got children?' The artificiality
of the situation threatened to bring on a bout of manic
laughter. It was surreal, sitting here making small talk
with a guy who probably hated her guts, even though,
thankfully, she had not been subjected to the sort of
blistering attack she had been fearing.

At least, not yet.

At any rate, she could always walk out…although he
had dangled that carrot in front of her, intimated that
he would indeed be willing to discuss the terms and
conditions of helping them. Could she seriously afford
to let her pride come in the way of some sort of solution to their problems?

If she had been the only one affected, then yes, but
there was her brother, her mother, those faithful employees left working, through loyalty, for poor salaries
in the ever-shrinking family business.

'This isn't about me,' Javier fielded silkily. 'Although, in answer to your question, I have reached the
conclusion that women, as a long-term proposition,
have no place in my life at this point in time. So, times
have changed for you,' he murmured, moving on with
the conversation. He reached into his drawer and extracted a sheet of paper, which he swivelled so that it
was facing her.

'Your company accounts. From riches to rags in the
space of a few years, although, if you look carefully,

you'll see that the company has been mismanaged for somewhat longer than a handful of years. Your dearly departed husband seems to have failed to live up to whatever promise there was that an injection of cash would rescue your family's business. I take it you were too busy playing the good little wife to notice that he had been blowing vast sums of money on pointless ventures that all crashed and burned?'

Sophie stared at the paper, feeling as though she had been stripped naked and made to stand in front of him for inspection.

'I knew,' she said abruptly. *Playing the good little wife?* How wrong could he have been?

'You ditched your degree course to rush into marriage with a man who blew the money on…oh, let's have a look…transport options for sustainable farmers…a wind farm that came to nothing…several aborted ventures into the property market…a sports centre which was built and then left to rot because the appropriate planning permission hadn't been provided… All the time your father's once profitable transport business was haemorrhaging money by the bucketload. And you knew…'

'There was nothing I could do,' Sophie said tightly, loathing him even though she knew that, if he were to lend them any money, he would obviously have to know exactly what he was getting into.

'Did you know where else your husband was blowing his money, to the tune of several hundred thousand?'

Perspiration broke out in a fine, prickly film and she stared at him mutinously.

'Why are you doing this?'

'Doing what?'

'Hanging me out to dry? If you don't want to help, then please just say so and I'll leave and you'll never see me again.'

'Fine.' Javier sat back and watched her.

She had never lain spread across his bed. He had never seen that hair in all its glory across his pillows. He had felt those ripe, firm breasts, but through prudish layers of clothes. He had never tasted them. Had never even *seen* them. Before he'd been able to do any of that, before he'd been able to realise the powerful thrust of his passion and his *yearning*, she had walked away from him. Walked straight up to the altar and into the arms of some little twerp whose very existence she had failed to mention in the months that they had been supposedly going out.

He had a sudden vision of her lying on his bed in the penthouse apartment, just one of several he owned in the capital. It was a blindingly clear vision and his erection was as fast as it was shocking. He had to breathe deeply and evenly in an attempt to dispel the unsettling and unwelcome image that had taken up residence in his head.

'Not going to walk out?' Javier barely recognised the raw lack of self-control that seemed to be guiding his responses.

He'd wanted to see her squirm but the force of his antipathy took him by surprise because he was realising just how fast and tight she had stuck to him over the years.

Unfinished business. That was why. Well, he would make sure he finished it if it was the last thing he did and then he would be free of the woman and whatever useless part of his make-up she still appeared to occupy.

'He gambled.' Sophie raised her eyes to his and held his stare in silence before looking away, offering him her averted profile.

'And you knew about that as well,' Javier had a fleeting twinge of regret that he had mentioned any of this. It had been unnecessary. Then he remembered the way she had summarily dumped him and all fleeting regret vanished in a puff of smoke.

She nodded mutely.

'And there was nothing you could have done about that either?'

'I don't suppose you've ever lived with someone who has a destructive addiction?' she said tightly. 'You can't just sit them down for a pep talk and then expect them to change overnight.'

'But you *can* send them firmly in the direction of professional help.' Javier was curious. The picture he had built of her had been one of the happily married young wife, in love with Prince Charming, so in love that she had not been able to abide being away from him whilst at university—perhaps hoping that the distraction of an unsuitable foreigner might put things into perspective, only for that gambit to hit the rocks.

Then, when he had inspected the accounts closely, he had assumed that, blindly in love, she had been ignorant of her loser husband's uncontrolled behaviour.

Now…

He didn't want curiosity to mar the purity of what he wanted from her and he was taken aback that it was.

'Roger was an adult. He didn't want help. I wasn't capable of manhandling him into a car and driving him to the local association for gambling addicts. And I don't want to talk about…about my marriage. I… It's in the past.'

'So it is,' Javier murmured. When he thought about the other man, he saw red, pure jealousy at being deprived of what he thought should have been his.

Crazy.

Since when had he considered any woman *his possession*?

'And yet,' he mused softly, 'when is the past ever *really* behind us? Don't you find that it dogs us like a guilty conscience, even when we would like to put it to bed for good?'

'What do you mean?'

'You ran out on me.'

'Javier, you don't *understand*…'

'Nor do I wish to. This isn't about understanding what motivated you.' And at this point in time—this very special point in time when the tables had been reversed, when she was now the one without money and he the one with the bank notes piled up in the coffers—well, she was hardly going to tell the whole truth and nothing but the truth when it came to motivations, was she? Oh, no, she would concoct some pretty little tale to try to elicit as much sympathy from him as she could…

'I'm not asking you to give me money, Javier. I…

I'm just asking for a loan. I would pay it all back, every penny of it.'

Javier flung back his head and laughed, a rich, full-bodied laugh that managed to lack genuine warmth. 'Really? I'm tickled pink at the thought of a Classics scholar, almost there but never graduated, and her sports scholarship brother running any company successfully enough to make it pay dividends, never mind a company that's on its last legs.'

'There *are* directors in the company...'

'Looked at them. I would ditch most of them if I were you.'

'You *looked at them*?'

Javier shrugged. His dark eyes never left her face. 'I probably know more about your company than you do. Why not? If I'm to sink money into it, then I need to know exactly what I will be sinking money into.'

'So...are you saying that you'll help?'

'I'll help.' He smiled slowly. 'But there's no such thing as a free lunch. There will be terms and conditions...'

'That's fine.' For the first time in a very long time, a cloud seemed to be lifting. She had underestimated him. He was going to help and she wanted to sob with relief. 'Whatever your terms and conditions, well, they won't be a problem. I promise.'

CHAPTER THREE

'Perhaps we should take this conversation somewhere else.'

'Why?' The suggestion of leaving with him for *somewhere else* sent little shivers of alarm skittering through her.

She could scarcely credit that she was sitting here, in this office, facing this man who had haunted her for years. All the things that had happened ever since that first tentative step as a young girl falling hopelessly in love with an unsuitable boy lay between them like a great, big, murky chasm.

There was just so much he didn't know.

But none of that was relevant. What was relevant was that he was going to help them and that was enough.

'Because,' Javier drawled, rising to his feet and strolling to fetch his jacket from where it lay slung over the back of one of the expensive, compact sofas in the little sitting area of the office, 'I feel that two old friends should not be discussing something as crass as a business bailout within the confines of an office.'

Two old friends?

Sophie scrutinised the harsh angles of his face for any inherent sarcasm and he returned her stare with bland politeness.

But his bland politeness made her feel unaccountably uneasy.

He'd never been polite.

At least, not in the way that English people were polite. Not in the middle-class way of clinking teacups and saying the right things, which was the way she had been brought up.

He had always spoken his mind and damned the consequences. She had occasionally seen him in action at university, once in the company of two of his lecturers, when they had been discussing economics.

He had listened to them, which had been the accepted polite way, but had then taken their arguments and ripped them to shreds. The breadth and depth of his knowledge had been so staggering that there had been no comeback.

He had never been scared of rocking the boat. Sometimes, she wondered whether he had privately relished it, although when she'd once asked him that directly, he had burst out laughing before kissing her senseless—at which point she had forgotten what she had been saying to him. Kissing him had always had that effect on her.

A surge of memories brought a hectic flush to her cheeks.

'Is this your new way of dressing?' he asked and Sophie blinked, dispelling disturbing images of when they had been an item.

'What do you mean?'

'You look like an office worker.'

'That's exactly what I am,' she returned lightly, following him to the door, because what else could she do? At this point, he held all the trump cards, and if he wanted to go and have their business chat sitting on bar stools in the middle of Threadneedle Street, then so be it. There was too much at stake for her to start digging her heels in and telling him that she felt more comfortable discussing business in an office.

She had come this far and there was no turning back now.

This floor was a sanctum of quiet. It was occupied by CEOs and directors, most of whom were concealed behind opaque glass and thick doors. In the middle there was a huge, open-plan space in which desks were cleverly positioned to allow for maximum space utilisation and minimum scope for chatting aimlessly.

The open space was largely empty, except for a couple of diligent employees who were too absorbed in whatever they were doing to look up at them as they headed for the directors' lift.

'But it's not exactly where you wanted to end up, is it?' he asked as the lift doors quietly closed, sealing them in together.

It didn't matter where she looked, reflections of him bounced back at her.

She shrugged and reluctantly met his dark eyes.

'You don't always end up where you think you're going to,' she said tersely.

'You had big plans to be a university lecturer.'

'Life got in the way of that.'

'I'm sure your dearly departed husband wouldn't like to be seen as someone who got in the way of your big plans.'

'I don't want to talk about Roger.'

Because the thought of him no longer being around was still too painful for her to bear. That thought struck Javier with dagger-like precision. The man might have been a waste of space when it came to business, and an inveterate gambler who had blown vast sums of money that should have been pumped into saving the company, yet she had loved him and now would have nothing said against him.

Javier's lips thinned.

He noted the way she scurried out of the lift, desperate to put some physical distance between them.

'When did you find out that the company was on the brink of going bust?'

Sophie cringed. She wanted to ask whether it was really necessary to go down that road and she knew that she had to divorce the past from the present. He wasn't the guy she had loved to death, the guy she had been forced to give up when life as she knew it had suddenly stopped. That was in the past and right now she was in the company of someone thinking about extending credit to the company. He would want details even if she didn't want to give them.

But there was a lot she didn't want to tell him. She didn't want his contempt or his pity and she knew she would have both if she presented him with the unadorned truth. That was if he believed her at all, which was doubtful.

'I knew things weren't too good a while back,' she said evasively. 'But I had no idea really of just how bad they were until…well, until I got married. '

Javier felt the dull, steady beat of jealousy working its poisonous way through his body.

He was painfully reminded of the folly of his youth, the naivety of imagining that they would have a future together. The poor foreigner working his way up and the beautiful, well-spoken, impeccably bred English girl who just so happened to be the apple of her father's adoring and protective eye.

At the time, he had thought himself to be as hard as nails and immune to distraction.

He'd set his course and he had been cocky enough to imagine that no ill winds would come along to blow him off target.

Of all the girls on the planet, he had found himself blown off target by one who had set her course on someone else and had been playing with him for a bit of fun, stringing him along while her heart belonged to someone else.

'And then…what?'

'What do you mean?' She nervously played with her finger, where once upon an unhappy time there had been a wedding ring.

She hadn't paid much attention to where they were going, but when he stood back to push open a door for her, she saw that they were at an old pub, the sort of pub that populated the heart of the City.

She shimmied past him, ducking under his out-stretched arm as he held the door open for her. She was tall at five foot ten, but he was several inches taller and she had a memory of how protected he had always made her feel. The clean, masculine scent of him lingered in her nostrils, making her feel shaky as she sat down at a table in the corner, waiting tensely while he went to get them something to drink. She knew she should keep a clear head and drink water but her nerves were all over the place. They needed something a little stronger than water.

Outside it was hot and she could glimpse a packed garden but in here it was cool, dark and relatively empty.

The sun worshippers were all drinking in the evening sun.

Trying to elicit details about her past was not relevant. Javier knew that and he was furious with himself for succumbing to the desire to know more.

Just like that, in a matter of minutes, she had managed to stoke his curiosity. Just like that, she was back under his skin and he couldn't wait to have her, to bed her, so that he could rid himself of the uncomfortable suspicion that she had been there all along, a spectre biding its time until it could resurface to catch him on the back foot.

For a man to whom absolute control was vital, this slither of susceptibility was unwelcome.

He realised that when he tried to think of the last woman he had slept with, a top-notch career woman in New York with legs to her armpits, he came up blank. He couldn't focus on anyone but the woman sitting in front of him, looking at him as though she expected him to pounce unexpectedly at any minute.

She had the clearest violet eyes he had ever seen, fringed with long, dark lashes, and the tilt of them gave her a slightly dreamy look, as though a part of her was on another plane. He itched to unpin her neat little bun so that he could see whether that glorious hair of hers was still as long, still as unruly.

'Well?' Javier demanded impatiently, hooking a chair with his foot and angling it so that he could sit with his long legs extended. He had brought a wine cooler with a bottle of wine and one of the bartenders placed two glasses in front of them, then simpered for a few seconds, doe-eyed, before reluctantly walking back to the bar.

'Well…what?'

'What was the order of events? Heady marriage, fairy-tale honeymoon and then, lo and behold, no more money? Life can be cruel. And where was your brother when all this was happening?'

'In America.' She sighed.

'By choice, even though he knew?' With the family company haemorrhaging money, surely it would have been an indulgence for Oliver to have stayed in California, enjoying himself…

'He didn't know,' Sophie said abruptly. 'And I don't know why…how all this is relevant.'

'I'm fleshing out the picture,' Javier said softly. 'You've come to me with a begging bowl. What did you think I was going to do? Give you a big, comforting hug and write out a cheque?'

'No, but…'

'Let's get one thing straight here, Sophie.' He leant forward and held her gaze. She couldn't have said a word even if she had wanted to. She could hardly breathe. 'You're here to ask a favour of me and, that being the case, whether you like it or not, you don't get to choose what questions to answer and what questions to ignore. Your private life is your business. Frankly, I don't give a damn. But I need to know your levels of capability when it comes to doing business. I need to know whether your brother is committed to working for the company, because if he was left to enjoy four years of playing sport in California, then I'm guessing he wouldn't have returned to the sick fold with a cheerful whistle. Most of the directors of the company aren't worth the money they're being paid.'

'You know how much they're being paid!'

'I know everything worth knowing about your crippled family company.'

'When did you get so…so…*hard*?'

Roughly around the same time I discovered what sort of woman I'd been going out with, Javier thought with the sour taste of cynicism in his mouth.

He leant back and crossed his legs, lightly cradling the stem of the wine glass between his long fingers.

'You don't make money by being a sap for sob stories,' he informed her coolly, keen eyes taking in the delicate bloom of colour in her cheeks. 'You've come to me with a sob story.' He shrugged. 'And the bottom line is this— if you don't like the direction this conversation is going, then, like I said before, you're free to go. But of course, we both know you won't, because you need me.'

He was enjoying this little game of going round the houses before he laid all his cards on the table, before she knew exactly what the terms and conditions of her repayment would be.

It wouldn't hurt her to realise just how dangerously close the company was to imploding.

It wouldn't hurt her to realise just how much she needed him…

'If you knew about your husband's hare-brained schemes and addiction to gambling, and you allowed it to go under the radar, then are you a trustworthy person to stand at the helm of your company?'

'I told you that there was nothing I could do,' she said with a dull flush.

'And if your brother was so clueless as to what was happening on the home front, then is *he* competent enough to do what would need to be done should I decide to help you out?'

'Ollie…doesn't have a huge amount of input in the actual running of things…'

'Why?'

'Because he's never been interested in the company and, yes, you're right—he's always resented the fact that he had to finally return to help out. He's found it difficult to deal with not having money.'

'And you've found it easy?'

'I've dealt with it.'

Javier looked at her narrowly and with a certain

amount of reluctant admiration for the streak of strength he glimpsed.

Not only had she had to face a tremendous fall from the top of the mountain, but the loss of her husband and the father she had adored.

Yet there was no self-pity in the stubborn tilt of her chin.

'You've had a lot to deal with, haven't you?' he murmured softly and she looked away.

'I'm no different from loads of people the world over who have found their lives changed in one way or another. And, now that you've got the measure of the company, will you lend us some money or not? I don't know if my brother told you, but the family house has been on the market for over two years and we just can't seem to sell it. There's no appetite for big houses. If we could sell it, then we might be able to cover some of the expenses…'

'Although a second mortgage was taken out on it…'

'Yes, but the proceeds would go a little way to at least fixing certain things that need urgent attention.'

'The dated computer systems, for example?'

'You really did your homework, didn't you? How did you manage that in such a small amount of time? Or have you been following my father's company over the years? Watching while it went downhill?'

'Why would I have done that?'

Sophie shrugged uncomfortably. 'I know you probably feel… Well, you don't understand what happened all those years ago.'

'Don't presume to think that you know what goes on

in my head, Sophie. You don't. And, in answer to your preposterous question, I haven't had the slightest clue what was going on in your father's company over the years, nor have I cared one way or the other.' He saw that the bottle was empty and debated whether or not to get another, deciding against it, because he wanted them both to have clear heads for this conversation.

When he knew that he would be seeing her, he had predicted how he would react and it hadn't been like this.

He'd thought that he would see her and would feel nothing but the acid, bilious taste of bitterness for having been played in the past and taken for a chump.

He'd accepted that she'd been in his head more than he'd ever imagined possible. A Pandora's box had been opened with her brother's unexpected appearance at his office. Javier had recognised the opportunity he had been given to put an end to her nagging presence, which, he now realised, had been embedded in him like a virus he'd never managed to shake off.

He would have her and he had the means to do so at his disposal.

She needed money. He had vast sums of it. She would take what was offered because she would have no choice. His *terms and conditions* would be met with acquiescence because, as he had learned over the years, money talked.

He had slept with some of the world's most desirable women. It had followed that whatever she had that had held him captive all those years ago, she would lose it when he saw her in the flesh once again. How could she compete with some of the women who had clamoured to sleep with him?

He'd been wrong.

And that was unbelievably frustrating because he was beginning to realise that he wanted a lot more from her than her body for a night or two.

No, he *needed* a lot more from her than her body for a night or two.

He wanted and needed *answers* and his curiosity to pry beneath the surface enraged him because he had thought himself above that particular sentiment when it came to her.

Nor, he was discovering, did he want to take what he knew she would have no choice but to give him in the manner of a marauding plunderer.

He didn't want her reluctance.

He wanted her to come to him and in the end, he reasoned now, if revenge was what he was after, then wouldn't that be the ultimate revenge? To have her want him, to take her and then to walk away?

The logical part of his brain knew that to want revenge was to succumb to a certain type of weakness, and yet the pull was so immensely strong that he could no more fight it than he could have climbed Mount Everest in bare feet.

And he was enjoying this.

His palate had become jaded and that was something he had recognised a while back, when he had made his first few million and the world had begun to spread itself out at his feet.

He had reached a place in life where he could have

whatever he wanted and sometimes having everything at your fingertips removed the glory of the chase. Not just women, but deals, mergers, money...the lot.

She wasn't at his fingertips.

In fact, she was simmering with resentment that she had been put in the unfortunate position of having to come to him, cap in hand, to ask for his help.

He was a part of her past that she would rather have swept under the carpet and left there. He was even forced to swallow the unsavoury truth that he was probably a part of her past she bitterly regretted ever having gone anywhere near in the first place.

But she'd wanted him.

That much he felt he knew. She might have played with him as a distraction from the main event happening in her life somewhere else, or maybe just to show off in front of her friends that she had netted the biggest fish in the sea—which Javier had known, without a trace of vanity, he was.

But perhaps she hadn't actually banked on the flare of physical attraction that had erupted between them. She had held out against him and he had seen that as shyness, youthful nerves at taking the plunge... He'd been charmed by it. He'd also been wrong about it, as it turned out. She'd held out against him because there had been someone else in her life.

But she'd still fancied him like hell.

She'd trembled when he'd traced his finger across her collarbone and her eyes had darkened when their lips had touched. He hadn't imagined those reactions. She might have successfully fought that attraction in the end and scurried back to her comfort zone, but, for a brief window, he'd taken her out of that comfort zone…

Did she imagine that she was now immune to that physical attraction because time had passed?

He played with the thought of her opening up to him like a flower and this time giving him what he had wanted all those years ago. What he wanted now.

He wondered what she would feel when she found herself discarded.

He wondered whether he would really care or whether the mere fact that he had had her would be sufficient.

He hadn't felt this *alive* in a long time and it was bloody great.

'I was surprised when your brother showed up on my doorstep, so to speak, in search of help.'

'I hope you know that I never asked him to come to see you.'

'I can well imagine, Sophie. It must cut to the quick having to beg favours from a man who wasn't good enough for you seven years ago.'

'That's not how it was.'

Javier held up one hand. 'But, as it happens, to see you evicted and in the poorhouse would not play well on my conscience.'

'That's a bit of an exaggeration, don't you think?'

'You'd be surprised how thin the dividing line is between the poor and the rich and how fast places can be swapped. One minute you're on top of the world, the ruler of everything around you, and the next minute you're lying on the scrap heap, wondering what went wrong. Or I could put it another way—one minute you're flying upwards, knocking back all those less fortunate cluttering your path, and the next minute you're spiralling downwards and the people you've knocked back are on their way up, having the last laugh.'

'I bet your parents are really sad at the person you've become, Javier.'

Javier flushed darkly, outraged at her remark, and even more outraged by the disappointed expression on her lovely face.

Of course, in those heady days of thinking she was his, he had let her into his world, haltingly confided in her in a way he had never done with any woman either before or since. He had told her about his background, about his parents' determination to make sure he left that life behind. He had painted an unadorned picture of life as he had known it, had been amused at the vast differences between them, had seen those differences as a good thing, rather than an unsurmountable barrier, as she had. If she'd even thought about it at all.

'I know you've become richer than your wildest dreams.' She smiled ruefully at him. 'And you always had very, very wild dreams…'

The conversation seemed to have broken its leash and was racing away in a direction Javier didn't like. He frowned heavily at her.

'And now here we are.'

'You once told me that all your parents wanted was for you to be happy, to make something of your life, to settle down and have a big family.'

Javier decided that he needed another drink after

all. He stood up abruptly, which seemed to do the trick, because she started, blinked and looked up at him as if suddenly remembering that she wasn't here for a trip down memory lane. Indeed, that a trip down memory lane was the very last thing she had wanted.

He'd forgotten that habit of hers.

He was barely aware of placing his order for another bottle of wine at the bar and ordering some bar snacks because they were now both drinking on fairly empty stomachs. He hadn't a clue what bar snacks he ordered, leaving it to the guy serving him to provide whatever was on the menu.

She was filling up his head. He could feel her eyes on him even as he stood here at the bar with his back to her.

Whatever memories he'd had of her, whatever memories he'd kidded himself he'd got rid of and had buried, he was now finding in a very shallow grave.

She'd always had that habit of branching out on a tangent. It was as if a stray word could spark some improbable connection in her head and carry her away down unforeseen paths.

There were no unforeseen paths in this scenario, he thought grimly as he made his way back to the table, where she was sitting with the guarded expression back on her face.

The only unforeseen thing—and it was something he could deal with—was how much he still wanted her after all this time.

'I should be getting back,' she said as he poured her a glass of wine and nodded to her to drink.

'I've ordered food.'

'My ticket…'

'Forget about your ticket.'

'I can't do that.'

'Why not?'

'Because I'm not made of money. In fact, I'm broke. There. Are you satisfied that I've said that? I can't afford to kiss sweet goodbye to the cost of the ticket to get me down here to London. You've probably forgotten how much train tickets cost, but if you'd like a reminder, I can show you mine. They cost a lot. And if you want to do a bit more gloating, then go right ahead.' She fluttered her hand wearily. 'I can't stop you.'

'You'll need to pare down the staff.'

'I beg your pardon?'

'The company is top-heavy. Too many chiefs and very few Indians.'

Sophie nodded. It was what she had privately thought but the thought of sitting down old friends of her parents and handing them their marching orders had been just too much to contemplate. Oliver couldn't have done that in a million years and, although she was a heck of a lot more switched on than he was, the prospect of sacking old retainers, even fairly ineffective old retainers, still stuck in her throat.

Few enough people had stuck by them through thin times.

'And you need to drag the business into this century. The old-fashioned transport business needs to be updated. You need to take risks, to branch out, to try to capture smaller, more profitable markets instead of sticking to having lumbering dinosaurs doing cross-

Channel deliveries. That's all well and good but you need a lot more than that if your company is to be rescued from the quicksand.'

'I…' She quailed at the thought of herself and Oliver, along with a handful of maybe or maybe not efficient directors, undertaking a job of those proportions.

'You and your brother are incapable of taking on this challenge,' Javier told her bluntly and she glared at him even though he had merely spoken aloud what she had been thinking.

'I'm sure if you agree to extend a loan,' she muttered, 'we can recruit good people who are capable of—'

'Not going to happen. If I sink money into that business of yours, I want to be certain that I won't be throwing my money into a black hole.'

'That's a bit unfair.' She fiddled with the bun which, instead of making her feel blessedly cool in the scorching temperatures, was making her sweaty and uncomfortable. As were the formal, scratchy clothes, so unlike her normal dress code of jeans, tee shirts and sneakers.

She didn't feel like the brisk, efficient potential client of someone who might want to extend a loan. She felt awkward, gauche and way too aware of the man looking at her narrowly, sizing her up in a way that made her want to squirm.

This wasn't the guy she had known and loved. He hadn't chucked her out of his office but, as far as feelings went, there was nothing there. There wasn't a trace of that simmering attraction that had held them both mesmerised captives all those years ago. He wasn't married but she wondered whether there was a woman in his life, someone rich and beautiful like him.

Even when he'd had no money, he could have had any woman he wanted.

Her mind boggled at the thought of how many women would now fall at his feet because he was the guy who had the full package.

A treacherous thought snaked into her head…

What if she'd defied her parents? What if she'd carried on seeing Javier? Had seen where that love might have taken them both?

It wouldn't have worked.

Despite the fact that she had grown up with money, had had a rich and pampered life, money per se was not what motivated her. For Javier, it was the only thing that motivated him.

She looked at him from under her lashes, taking in the cut of his clothes, the hand-tailored shoes, the mega-expensive watch around which dark hair curled. He *breathed* wealth. It was what made him happy and made sense of his life.

She might be stressed out because of all the financial worries happening in her life, but if those worries were removed and she was given a clean slate, then she knew that she wouldn't really care if that slate was a rich slate or not.

So, if she'd stayed with him, she certainly wouldn't have been the sort of woman he'd have wanted. She might talk the talk but her jeans, tee shirts and sneakers would not have been found acceptable attire.

They'd had their moment in time when they'd both

been jeans and tee shirts people but he'd moved on, and he would always have moved on.

The attraction, for him, would have dimmed and finally been snuffed out.

The road she'd taken had been tough and miserable and, as things had turned out, the wrong one. But it would be silly to think that she would have been any happier if she'd followed Javier and held the hand he'd extended.

'We can go round the houses discussing what's fair and what's unfair,' he said in a hard voice. 'But that won't get us anywhere. I'm prepared to sink money in, but I get a cut of the cake and you abide by my rules.'

'Your rules?' She looked at him in bewilderment.

'Did you really think I'd write a cheque and then keep my fingers crossed that you might know what to do with the money?' He'd had one plan when this situation had first arisen—it had been clean and simple—but now he didn't want clean and simple. He needed to get more immersed in the water…and he was looking forward to that.

'I will, to spell it out, want a percentage of your business. There's no point my waiting for the time when you can repay me. I already have more money than I can shake a stick at, but I could put your business to some good use, branch out in ways that might dovetail with some of my other business concerns.'

Sophie shifted, not liking the sound of this. If he wanted a part of their business, wouldn't that involve him *being around*? Or was he talking about being a silent partner?

'Does your company have a London presence at all?'

Javier was thoroughly enjoying himself. Who said the only route to satisfaction was getting what you wanted on demand? He'd always been excellent when it came to thinking outside the box. He was doing just that right now. Whatever he sank into her business would be peanuts for him but he could already see ways of turning a healthy profit.

And as for having her? Of course he would, but where was the rush after all? He could take a little time out to relish this project...

'Barely,' she admitted. 'We closed three of the four branches over the years to save costs.'

'And left one open and running?'

'We couldn't afford to shut them all...even though the overheads are frightening.'

'Splendid. As soon as the details are formalised and all the signatures are in place, I will ensure that the office is modernised and ready for occupation.'

'It's already occupied,' Sophie said, dazed. 'Mandy works on reception and twice a week one of the accountants goes down to see to the various bits of post. Fortunately nearly everything is done by email these days...'

'Pack your bags, Sophie. I'm taking up residence in your London office, just as soon as it's fit for habitation, and you're going to be sitting right there alongside me.'

Not quite the original terms and conditions he had intended to apply, but in so many ways so much better...

CHAPTER FOUR

'I DON'T KNOW what you're so worried about. His terms and conditions seem pretty fair to me. In fact, better than fair. He's going to have a percentage interest in the company but at least it'll be a company that's making money.'

That had been Oliver's reaction when she had presented him, a fortnight ago, with the offer Javier had laid out on the table for her to take or reject.

He had been downright incredulous that she might even be hesitating to eat from the hand that had been extended to feed her. In a manner that was uncharacteristically proactive for him, he had called an extraordinary meeting of the directors and presented them with Javier's plan, and Sophie had had to swallow the unpalatable reality that her past had caught up with her and was now about to join hands with her present.

Since then, with papers signed and agreements reached at the speed of light, the little office they had kept open in Notting Hill had been awash with frantic activity.

Sophie had refused to go. She had delegated that task to her brother, who had been delighted to get out of

Yorkshire for a couple of weeks. He had reported back with gusto at the renovations being made and, inside, Sophie had quailed at the way she felt, as though suddenly her life was being taken over.

She knew she was being ridiculous.

Javier had agreed to see them because of their old connection but there had been nothing there beyond that historic connection. He had made no attempts to pursue any conversations about what had happened between them. He had been as cool as might have been expected given the circumstances of their break-up and she was in no doubt that the only reason he had agreed to help them was because he could see a profit in what was being offered.

Money was what he cared about and she suspected that he would be getting a good deal out of them. They were, after all, in the position of the beggars who couldn't be choosers.

Hadn't he greeted her with all the information he had accumulated about the company?

He had done his homework and he wouldn't be offering them a rescue package if he wasn't going to get a great deal out of it.

She brushed her skirt, neatened her blouse and inspected herself in the mirror in the hallway, but she wasn't really seeing her reflection. She was thinking, persuading herself that his attitude towards her made everything much easier. For him, the past was history. What he had with her now was a business deal and one that had fallen into his lap like a piece of ripe fruit that hadn't even needed plucking from the tree.

Maybe in some distant corner of his mind there was an element of satisfaction that he was now in a position to be the one calling the shots, but if that was the case, he would have to have cared one way or another about her and he didn't.

The effect he still had on her was not mutual. And even her responses to him were an illusion, no more than a reminder of the power of nostalgia, because truthfully her heart was safely locked away, never again to be taken out to see the light of day.

She blinked and focused on the tidy image staring back at her. Everything in place. In a few minutes the taxi would come to take her to the station. A month ago, she would have hit the bus stop, which was almost a mile away, but he had deposited a large advance of cash in the company account to cover expenses and to ensure that everyone on the payroll was compensated for the overtime which they had contributed over the months and which had not been paid.

She would take the taxi to the station and then the train down to London so that she could see the final, finished product, the newly refurbished offices in which she would be stationed for as long as it took to get things up and running.

'How long do you think that's going to take?' she had asked Javier on day one, heart thumping at the prospect of being in an office where, on a whim, he could descend without warning.

He had shrugged, his dark-as-night eyes never leaving her face. 'How long is a piece of string? There's a lot of work to do with the company before it begins to pull its weight. There's been mass wastage of money and resources, expenditures that border on criminal and incompetent staff by the bucketload.'

'And you're going to…er…be around, supervising…?'

His eyes had narrowed on her flushed face. 'Does the prospect of that frighten you, Sophie?'

'Not in the slightest,' she had returned quickly. 'I would just be surprised if you managed to take time off from being the ruler of all you surveyed to help out an ailing firm. I mean, don't you have minions who move in when you take over sick companies?'

'I think I might give the minions a rest on this particular occasion,' he had murmured softly.

'Why?' Sophie had heard the thread of desperation in her voice. She couldn't be within five feet of him without her body reliving the way he had once made it feel, playing stupid games with her mind.

'This is a slightly more personal venture for me, Sophie,' he had told her, leaning across the boardroom table where both of them had remained after the legal team had exited. 'Maybe I want to see that the job is done to the highest possible standard given our…past acquaintanceship.'

Sophie hadn't known whether to thank him or quiz him, so she had remained silent, her eyes helplessly drifting down to his sensual mouth before sliding away as heat had consumed her.

With a little sigh, she grabbed her handbag as she heard the taxi circle the gravelled forecourt, and then she was on her way, half hoping that Javier wouldn't be there waiting at the office when she finally arrived, half hoping that he might be, and hating herself for that weakness.

She had no idea what to expect to find. The last time she had visited this particular office had been two years previously, when she and Oliver had been trying to decide which of the offices to shut. She remembered it as spacious enough but, without any money having been spent on it at all, it had already been showing telltale signs of wear and tear. That said, it had been the biggest and the least run-down, so they'd been able to amalgamate the diminishing files and folders there from the other offices.

Not for the first time, as she was ferried from north to south, she thought about how clueless she had been about the groundbreaking changes that had been happening right under her nose.

Ollie, at least, had had the excuse of being abroad, because he had left on his sports scholarship two years before she had gone to Cambridge. He'd been a fresh-faced teenager wrapped up in his own life, with no vision of anything happening outside it.

But she had still been living at home, in her final years at school. Why hadn't she asked more probing questions when her mother's health had begun to fail? The doctor had talked about stress, and now Sophie marvelled that she hadn't dug deeper to find out what the stress had been all about, because on the surface her mother could not have been living a less stressed-out life.

And neither had she questioned the frequency with which Roger's name had cropped up in conversations or the number of times he'd been invited along to the house for various parties. She had been amused at his enthusiasm and had eventually drifted into going out with him; she had never suspected the amount of encouragement he had got from her parents.

All told, she had allowed herself to be wrapped up in cotton wool. So when that cotton wool had been cruelly yanked off, she had been far more shell-shocked than she might otherwise have been.

Everything had hit her at once. She had been bombarded from all sides and, in the middle of this, had had to wise up quickly to the trauma of discovering just how ill her father was and the lengths he had gone to to protect them all from knowing.

She should have been there helping out long before the bomb had detonated, splintering shrapnel through their lives.

If she had been, then perhaps the company could have taken a different direction. And, if it had taken a different direction, then she wouldn't be here now, at the mercy of a guy who could still send her senses reeling, whatever her head was telling her.

Once in London, Sophie took a black cab to the premises of the office in Notting Hill.

Oliver had told her that things were coming along brilliantly but he had undersold just how much had been done in the space of a few days. It wasn't just about the paint job on the outside or the impressive potted plants or the newly painted black door with its gold lettering announcing the name of the company.

Standing back, Sophie's mouth fell open as she took

in the smart exterior. Then the door opened and she was staring at a casually dressed Javier, who, in return, stared back at her as he continued to lounge indolently against the door frame. Arms folded, he was already projecting the signs of ownership so that, as she took a few tentative steps towards him, she felt herself to be the visitor.

'Wow.' She hovered, waiting for him to step back, which he did after a couple of seconds, taking his time to unfold his gloriously elegant body and then stand aside so that she had to brush past him, immediately turning around and establishing a safe physical distance between them. 'It's completely changed on the outside.'

'There's no point having an office that repels potential clients,' Javier said drily.

Yet again, she was in work attire. The sort of clothes that drained her natural beauty.

'Why have you shown up wearing a suit?' he asked, strolling past her and expecting her to follow, which she duly did. 'And where is your bag? You do realise that you will be relocating to London for the foreseeable future?'

'I've been giving that some thought...'

Javier stopped and turned to look at her. 'Forget it.'

'I beg your pardon?'

'Remember the terms and conditions? One of them is that you relocate down here so that you can oversee the running of the London arm of the business.'

'Yes, but—'

'No *buts*, Sophie.' His voice was cool and unyielding. He hooked his fingers on the waistband of his black jeans, which sat low on his lean hips, and held her stare. 'You don't get to dip in and out of this. You're on the letterhead, along with your brother, and of course myself. Don't think that you're going to reap the rewards without doing any of the hard graft. I intend to oversee proceedings initially but I need to be assured that you and your brother won't run the company back into the ground the second my back's turned. Don't forget, this isn't a charity gesture of goodwill on my part. I'm not parting with cash if I don't think that there will be a decent return on my investment.'

Sophie thought that she'd been right. It was all about the money for him. Yes, there was a personal connection, but the animosity of their break-up wasn't paramount in his decision to help them. What mattered was that he was being handed a potentially very profitable business with an age-old reputation at a very cheap price because she and Oliver were desperate.

She imagined that, once the company was sorted, its reputation would not only be repaired but would ensure gold-plated business and a return of all the customers they had sadly lost over the years.

Right now, Oliver had an interest in a third of the company, but he would quickly lose interest and, she foresaw, would cash in his shares, take the money and head back to California, where he could continue his sporting career in a teaching capacity.

In due course, Javier would have invested in a very worthwhile project at a very good price.

And their past history did not figure in the calculations. In fact, she wondered whether he felt anything at all about what had happened between them.

'I thought I might commute down.'

Javier burst out laughing before sobering up to look at her with a gimlet-eyed warning. 'I wouldn't even entertain that notion if I were you,' he informed her in the sort of voice that did not expect contradiction. 'In the first few weeks there will probably be a great deal of overtime, and hopping on and off a train to try to get the work done just isn't going to cut it.'

'I have nowhere to stay here.' Once upon a time, there had been a snazzy apartment in Kensington but, she had discovered, that had been mortgaged up to the hilt when the company had started shedding customers and losing profit. It had been sold ages ago.

'Your brother has stayed in a hotel when he's been down.' Javier's eyes roved over her flushed face. 'But,' he mused with soft speculation, 'as you're going to be here for considerably longer, I have already made arrangements for you to have use of one of my apartments in Notting Hill. You'll be within convenient walking distance of the company. No excuse for slacking off.'

'No!' She broke out in clammy perspiration.

'Reason being…?'

'I…I can't just decamp down here to London, Javier!'

'This isn't something that's open to debate.'

'You don't understand.'

'Then enlighten me.' They hadn't even stepped foot into the renovated office and already they were arguing.

He couldn't credit that he had originally played with the thought of helping her in return for having her. He couldn't think of anything less satisfying than having her blackmailed into coming to him as a reluctant and resentful partner when he wanted her hot, wet and willing...

He also couldn't credit that he had simplistically imagined that one scratch would ease this itch that had surfaced with such surprising speed the second her brother had opened that door back into the past. The more he saw of her, the more he *thought* of her, the more dangerously deep his unfinished business with her felt. One or two nights wasn't going to be enough.

'I have to keep an eye on the house,' she said with obvious reluctance.

'What house?'

'The family home.'

'Why? Is it in imminent danger of falling down if you're not at hand with some sticking plaster and masking tape?'

Bitter tears sprang to her eyes and she fought them down as a red mist of anger swirled through her in a tidal rush.

'Since when did you get so arrogant?' she flung at him. They stared at one another in electric silence before she broke eye contact to storm off, out of the beautiful reception area, which she had barely noticed at all, and into the first set of offices.

It took a couple of seconds before Javier was galvanised into following her.

Being accused of *arrogance* was not something he was accustomed to. Indeed, being spoken to in that accusatory, critical tone of voice was unheard of. He

caught her arm, tugging her to face him and then immediately releasing her because just the feel of her softness
under his fingers was like putting his hand against an
open flame. It enraged him that she could still have this
effect on him. It enraged him that, for the first time in
living memory, and certainly for the first time in many,
many years, his body was refusing to obey his mind.

'Are you sure it's the house you need to be close
to?' he growled.

'What are you talking about?'

'Maybe there's a man lurking in the background...'
Javier was disgusted to realise that he was fishing. Did
he care whether there was some lame boyfriend in the
background? She wasn't married and that was the main
thing. He would never have gone near any woman with
a wedding ring on her finger, but if she had a boyfriend
somewhere, another one of those limp ex–public school
idiots who thought that a polished accent was all that it
took to get you through life, well...

All was fair in love and war...

Sophie reddened. The dull prickle of unpleasant
memories tried to surface and she resolutely shoved
them back where they belonged, in the deepest corners of her mind.

'Because, if you have, then he'll just have to take
a back seat for...however long it takes. And word of
warning—my apartment is for sole occupation only...'

'You mean if there was a guy in my life, and I happened to be living in one of your apartments, I wouldn't
be allowed to entertain him?'

Javier looked at her appalled expression and swatted away the uncomfortable feeling that he was being pigeon-holed as some kind of dinosaur when that couldn't have been further from the truth. Having reached the soaring heights the hard way, he made a conscious effort to ensure that the employees of his company were hand-picked for all the right reasons: talent, merit and ability. He made sure that there were no glass ceilings for women, or for those who had had to struggle to find their way, as he had.

He was not the sort of guy who would ever have dreamt of laying down pathetic rules about men being kept apart from women, like teenagers in boarding schools overseen by strict house masters.

So what was he doing right now? And how was it that he had no intention of doing otherwise?

'I mean you're probably going to be working long hours. The distraction of some man who wants you back home to cook his meal by five-thirty isn't going to work' was the most he would offer.

Sophie laughed shortly. If only he knew...

'There's no man around to distract me,' she said in a low voice. 'And, yes, as a matter of fact the house *is* falling down, and Oliver won't be there because he's been dispatched to France to see what's happening to the company over there...'

'Your house is falling down?'

'Not literally,' Sophie admitted. 'But there's a lot wrong with it and I'm always conscious of the fact that if it springs a leak and I'm not there to sort it out, well...'

'Since when has your house been falling down?'

'It doesn't matter.' She sighed and began to run her fingers through her hair, only to realise that she had pinned it up, and let her hand drop to her side. She looked around her but was very much aware of his eyes still on her, and even more aware that somehow they were now standing way too close for comfort.

'You've done marvellous things with the space.' She just wanted to get away from the threat of personal quizzing. She took a few steps away from him and now took time really to notice just how much *had* been done. It was not just a paint job; everything seemed very different from what she remembered.

It seemed much, much larger and that, she realised, was because the space within the first-floor office block had been maximised. Partitions had been cleverly put in where before there had been none. The dank carpeting had been replaced with wooden floors. The desks and furniture were all spanking new. She listened and nodded as he explained the dynamics of the place being manned and who should be working the London office. The client list would have to be updated. The sales team would need to be far more assertive. He had identified useful gaps in the market that could be exploited.

Everything was perfect. There were two private offices and she would be occupying one. Again she nodded because, like it or not, she was going to be here, in London.

'But,' she said when the tour had been concluded and they were in the pristine, updated kitchen, sitting at the high-tech beaten metallic table with cups of steaming coffee in front of them, 'I still don't feel comfortable leaving the house and I don't want to live in one of your apartments.' *He would have a key... He would be able to walk in unannounced at any given time... She could be in the shower and he could just stroll in...*

Her nipples tightened, pushing against her lacy bra and sending tingles up and down, in and out and through her from her toes to her scalp. She licked her lips and reminded herself that if he felt anything towards her at all it would be loathing because of what had happened between them in the past. Although, in reality, he couldn't even be bothered to feel such a strong emotion. What he felt was…indifference.

So if he were to let himself in, which he most certainly wouldn't, the shower would be the last place he would seek her out. Her responses were all over the place and it wouldn't be long before he started to realise that she wasn't as immune to him as she was desperately trying to be.

'I'll bring your brother back over.'

'No! Don't…'

'Why not?' Javier raised his eyebrows expressively, although he knew the reason well enough. Oliver didn't want to be stuck in Yorkshire and he didn't see his future with the family business. He resented the penury into which they had been thrust and, although he recognised the importance of rebuilding what had fallen into disrepair, he really thought no further than what that personally meant for him. Given half a chance, he would have cashed in his shares and headed for the hills. In due course he would, which would be interesting should Javier decide he wanted more than he had.

That was unlikely, because once he was done with getting what he wanted, he would be more than happy to disappear and leave the running of the business to an underling of his choice.

'He's enjoying being in Paris.'

'And that's how it's always been, isn't it?' Javier asked softly and Sophie raised translucent violet eyes to look at him with a frown.

'What do you mean?'

'I remember how you used to talk about your twin.' He had resolved not to go down any maudlin, reminiscing roads but now found that he couldn't help himself. 'The party animal. Off to California while you stayed behind to do your A levels. Praised for being sporty and indulged at a time when most kids that age would have had their head in textbooks to make sure they passed exams. When he came down to see you, he barely stayed put. He managed to make friends in five seconds and then off he went to see what nightclubs there were. He had his fun, enjoyed Mummy and Daddy's money and never had to face up to any grim realities because by then he was in California on his sports scholarship...

'I bet no one ever filled him in about the reality of the company losses, not even you...not even when they were glaringly obvious. I'll bet he only found out the extent of the trouble when you couldn't hide it from him any longer. Did your beloved ex-husband likewise conspire to keep your immature brother in the dark?'

'I told you.' Sophie stiffened at the mention of her ex-husband. 'I don't want to talk about Roger.'

Javier's lips tightened. The more she shied away from all mention of her ex, the more his curiosity was piqued. He was bitterly reminded of his pointless *wondering* when she had dumped him, when she had told him that she was destined to marry someone else... When she had married a guy whom he had found himself researching on the Internet even though it had been an exercise in masochism.

He had learned strength from a very young age. It had taken a great deal of willpower to avoid the pitfalls of so many of his friends when he had been growing up in poverty in Spain. The easy way out had always been littered with drugs and violence, and that easy way had been the popular route for many of the kids he had known. He had had to become an island to turn his back on all of that, just as he had had to develop a great deal of inner strength when he had finally made it to England to begin his university career. He had had to set his sights on distant goals and allow himself to be guided only by them.

Sophie had taken his eye off the ball, and here she was, doing it again.

The sooner he got her out of his system, the better.

'So your brother stays in Paris,' he said, with the sort of insistence that made her think of steamrollers slowly and inexorably flattening vast swathes of land. 'I could get someone to house-sit and daily look for walls falling down...'

'You might think it's funny, Javier, but it's not. You might live in your mansion now, and you might be able to get whatever you want at the snap of a finger, but it's just not funny when you have to watch every step you take because there might just be a minefield waiting to explode if you put your foot somewhere wrong. And I'm surprised you have no sympathy at all, considering you...you were...'

'I was broke? Penniless? A poor immigrant still trying to get a grip on the first rung of that all-important ladder? I feel it's fair to say that our circumstances were slightly different.'

'And, in a way, you probably have no idea how much worse it makes it for me.' She swung her head away. Her prissy, formal clothes felt like a straitjacket and her tidy bun nestled at the nape of her neck was sticky and restricting.

Without thinking, she released it and sifted restless fingers through the length of her tumbling hair.

And Javier watched. His mouth went dry. Her hair cascaded over her shoulders and down her back, a vibrant wash of colour that took his breath away. He had to look away but he knew that he was breathing fast, imagining her naked, projecting how her body would feel were he to run his hands along its shapely contours.

'You're right. Oliver has always been protected,' she told him bluntly. He might very well be the first person she was telling this to. It was a truth she had always kept to herself because to have voiced it would have felt like a little betrayal. 'He only found out about... everything when Dad's illness was finally revealed, and even then we didn't tell him that the company was on its last legs. In fact, he returned to California and only came back after the...the accident when... Well, he came back for Dad's funeral, and of course Roger's, and by then he had to be told.

'But his heart isn't in getting the company up and running. His heart isn't in the house either. Mum's now living in Cornwall and, as far as Ollie is concerned, he would sell the family home to the highest bidder if there was anyone around who was in the slightest bit interested. He doesn't give a hoot if it all falls down in a pile of rubble just so long as we got some money for the rubble. So, no, he wouldn't be at all happy to leave Paris to house-sit.'

She took a deep, shaky breath. 'The house hasn't been maintained for years. It always looked good on the outside, not that I ever really *looked*, but it turned out that there were problems with the roof and subsidence that had never been sorted. There's no money left in the pot to sort that stuff out, so I keep my eyes peeled for anything that might need urgent attention. The worse the house is, the less money we'll get, if we ever manage to sell at all. I can't afford for a leak to spring in the cellar and start mounting the stairs to the hallway.' She sighed and rubbed her eyes.

'Why did you let him get away with it?' It was more of a flat, semi-incredulous statement than a question and Sophie knew exactly who he was talking about even though no name had been mentioned.

'I don't want to talk about that. It's in the past and there's no point stressing about the stuff you can't change. I just have to deal with the here and now...'

'Oliver,' Javier ploughed on, 'might be indifferent and clueless when it comes to business, but you clearly have the capacity to get involved, so why didn't you? You knew what was happening.'

'Mum wasn't in good health. Hadn't been for ages. And then Dad's behaviour started getting weird... erratic... Suddenly everything seemed to be happening at the same time. We found out just how ill he was and then, hard on the heels of that, the full repercussions of...of Roger's gambling and all the bad investments began coming to light. There was no one at the helm. All the good people were leaving. Lots had already left, although I didn't know that at the time, because I'd never been involved in the family business. It was...chaos.'

Even in the midst of this tale of abject woe, Javier couldn't help but notice that there was no condemnation of her scoundrel husband. Loyalties, he thought with a sour taste, were not divided.

'So I'll get a house-sitter,' he repeated and she shook her head. He had already infiltrated her life enough. She wasn't sure she could cope with more.

'I'll come here,' she conceded, 'and go home at the weekends.' She breathed in deeply. 'And thank you for the use of an apartment. You have to let me know... I don't have a great deal of disposable income, as you can imagine, but please let me know how much rent I will owe you.'

Javier sat back and looked at her from under sinfully long lashes, a lazy, speculative look that felt like a caress.

'Don't even think of paying me rent,' he told her silkily. 'It's on the house...for old times' sake. Trust me,

Sophie, I want you…' he paused fractionally '…there at the helm while changes are taking place, and what I want, I usually get…whatever the cost.'

CHAPTER FIVE

SOPHIE LOOKED AROUND her and realised guiltily that, after two weeks' living in the apartment Javier had kindly loaned her, refusing to countenance a penny in payment, she was strangely *happy*.

The apartment was to die for. She still found herself admiring the décor, as she was doing right now, having just returned from the office and kicked off her stupid pumps so that she could walk barefoot on the cool, wooden floor.

She had expected minimalist with lots of off-putting glossy white surfaces, like the inside of a high-tech lab. Images of aggressive black leather and chrome everywhere had sprung to mind when she had been handed the key to the apartment by his personal assistant, who had accompanied her so that the workings of the various gadgets could be explained.

She had assumed that she would be overwhelmed by an ostentatious show of wealth, would be obliged to gasp appropriately at furnishings she didn't really like and would feel like an intruder in a foreign land.

The Javier of today was not the teasing, warm, sexy,

funny guy she had once known. The today Javier was tough, rich beyond most people's wildest dreams, ruthless and cutting edge in his hand-tailored suits and Italian shoes. And that would be reflected in any apartment he owned.

She'd been surprised—shocked, even—when she was shown the apartment.

'It's had a makeover,' the personal assistant had said in a vaguely puzzled voice, but obviously far too well-trained to comment further. 'So this is the first time I'm seeing the new version…'

Sophie hadn't quizzed her on what it had been like previously. Tired and in need of updating, she had assumed. He'd probably bought a bunch of apartments without even seeing them, the way you do when you have tons of money, and then paid someone handsomely to turn them into the sort of triple-A, gold-plated investments that would rent for a small fortune and double in value if he ever decided to sell.

Whoever had done the interior design had done a great job.

She padded towards the kitchen, which was cool, in shades of pale grey with vintage off-white tiles on the floor and granite counters that matched the floor.

Everything was open-plan. She strolled into the living room with a cup of tea and sank into the cosy sofa, idly flicking on the television to watch the early-evening news.

It was Friday and the work clothes had been dumped in the clothes hamper. Javier had told her that it was fine to dress casually but she had ignored him.

Keep it professional; keep it businesslike... she had decided.

Jeans and tee shirts would blur the lines between them...at least for her...

Not, in all events, that it made a scrap of difference how she dressed, because, after the first day, he had done a disappearing act, only occasionally emailing her or phoning her for updates. A couple of times he had visited the branch when she had been out seeing customers, trying to drum up business, and she could only think that he had timed his arrivals cleverly to avoid bumping into her.

He didn't give a passing thought to her, whilst she, on the other hand, couldn't stop thinking about him.

She didn't think that she had ever really stopped thinking about him. He'd been in her head, like the ghost of a refrain from a song that wouldn't go away.

And now she couldn't stop thinking about him. Worse than that, she spent every day at the office anticipating his unexpected arrival and was disproportionately disappointed when five-thirty rolled round and he'd failed to make an appearance.

Her heart skipped a beat when she opened up her emails and found a message from him waiting for her.

Her throat went dry when she heard the deep, sexy timbre of his voice on the end of the line.

She was in danger of obsessing over a guy who belonged to her past. At least, emotionally.

He'd suddenly reappeared on the scene, opening all sorts of doors in her head, making her think about choices she had made and bringing back memories of the horror story that had followed those choices.

He made her think about Roger. He was curious about her ex. She sensed that. Perhaps not curious in a personal way, but mildly curious, especially because so many things didn't quite add up. Why, he had asked her, hadn't she intervened when she'd known that he was blowing vast sums of money gambling? When she'd discovered the scale of the financial problems with the company? Why hadn't she acted more decisively?

But, of course, that was the kind of person he was. Someone who was born and bred to act decisively. He could never begin to understand how easy it was just to get lost and find yourself in a fog, with no guiding lights to lead you out.

She had grown up a lot since then. She had had to. And, in the process of taking charge, she had realised just how feeble her brother was when it came to making decisions and taking difficult paths.

When she looked back at herself as she had been seven years ago, it was like staring at a stranger. The carefree girl with a life full of options was gone for ever. She was a woman now with limited options and too many bad memories to deal with.

Was that why she was now obsessing over Javier, someone she had known for such a short space of time? Was it because he reminded her of the girl she used to be? Was it obsession by association, so to speak?

He made her think things she would rather have forgotten but he also made her heart skip a beat the way it once used to when she'd been with him.

And more than that, he made her body feel alive the way it hadn't for years. Not since him, in fact. He made her feel young again and that had a very seductive appeal.

With an impatient click of her tongue, she raised the volume of the television, determined not to waste the evening thinking about Javier and remembering what life had been like when they had been going out.

She almost didn't hear the buzz of the doorbell, and when she did, she almost thought that she might have made a mistake because no one could possibly be calling on her.

Since she had moved to London, she had kept herself to herself. She knew a couple of people who had relocated from the northern branch but the London crew, all very able and super-efficient, were new and she had shied away from making friends with any of them.

For starters, although it wasn't advertised and in all probability none of them knew, she was more or less their boss. And also…did she really want anyone knowing her backstory? It was just easier to maintain a healthy distance, so there was no way whoever had buzzed her from downstairs was a colleague on the hunt for a Friday night companion.

She picked up the intercom which allowed her to see her unexpected visitor and the breath left her in a whoosh.

'You're in.' Javier had come to the apartment on the spur of the moment. Since she'd started at the London office, he had seen her once, had spoken to her six times and had emailed her every other day. He had purposefully kept his distance because the strength of his response to her had come as a shock. Accustomed to having absolute control over every aspect of his life, he had assumed that her sudden appearance in his highly ordered existence would prove interesting—certainly rewarding, bearing in mind he intended to finish what had been started seven years previously—and definitely nothing that he wouldn't be able to handle.

Except that, from the very minute he had laid eyes on her, all that absolute certainty had flown through the window. The easy route he had planned to take had almost immediately bitten the dust. He'd had every intention of coolly trading his financial help for the body he had been denied, the body he discovered he still longed to touch and explore.

She'd used him and now he'd been given a golden opportunity to get his own back.

Except, he'd seen her, and that approach had seemed worse than simplistic. It had seemed crass.

There was no way he was going to pursue her and showing up at the workplace every day would have smelled a lot like pursuit, even though he had every right to be there, considering the amount of money he was sinking into the failing company.

He wanted her to come to him but staying away had been a lot more difficult than he'd dreamed possible.

Like someone dying of thirst suddenly denied the glass of ice-cold water just within his reach, he had found himself thinking about her to the point of distraction, and that had got on his nerves.

So here he was.

Sophie frantically wondered whether she could say that she was just on her way out. His unexpected appearance had brought her out in a nervous cold sweat. She had been thinking about him, and here he was, conjured up from her imagination.

'I...I...'

'Let me in.'

'I was just about to...have something to eat, actually...'

'Perfect. I'll join you.'

That wasn't what she'd had in mind. What she'd had in mind was a lead-up to a polite excuse and an arrangement to meet when she had some sort of defence system in place. Instead, here she was, hair all over the place, wearing jogging bottoms and an old, tight tee shirt bought at a music festival a dozen years ago and shrunk in the wash over time.

'Come on, Sophie! I'm growing older by the minute!'

'Fine!' She buzzed him in, belatedly remembering that it was actually *his* apartment, so he had every right to be here. And not only was it *his* apartment, but she wasn't paying a penny towards the rent, at his insistence.

She scrambled to the mirror by the front door, accepted that it was too late to start pinning her hair back into something sensible, and even though she was expecting him, she still started when he rapped on the door.

He'd obviously come straight from work, although, *en route*, he had divested himself of his tie, undone the top couple of buttons of his shirt and rolled his sleeves to his elbows. Her eyes dipped to his sinewy forearms and just as quickly back to his face.

'You look flustered,' Javier drawled, leaning against the door frame and somehow managing to crowd her. 'I haven't interrupted you in the middle of something pressing, have I?' This was how he remembered her. Tousled and sexy and so unbelievably, breathtakingly *fresh*.

And *innocent*.

Which was a bit of a joke, all things considered.

Dark eyes drifted downwards, taking in the outline of her firm, round breasts pushing against a tee shirt that was a few sizes too small, taking in the slither of flat belly where the tee shirt ended and the shapeless jogging bottoms began. Even in an outfit that should have done her no favours, she still looked hot, and his body responded with suitable vigour.

He straightened, frowning at the sudden discomfort of an erection.

'I haven't managed to catch much of you over the past couple of weeks.' He dragged his mind away from thoughts of her, a bed and a heap of hurriedly discarded clothes on the ground. 'So I thought I'd try you at home before you disappeared up north for the weekend.'

'Of course.'

There was a brief pause, during which he tilted his head to one side, before pointedly looking at the door handle.

'So...' He looked around him at his apartment with satisfaction. He'd had it redone. 'How are you finding the apartment?'

Some might say that he'd been a little underhand in the renovating of the apartment, which had been in perfectly good order a month previously. He'd walked round it, looking at the soulless, sterile furnishings, and had been able to picture her reaction to her new surroundings: disdain. He had always been amused at her old-fashioned tastes, despite the fact that she had grown up with money.

'I imagine your family home to be a wonder of the most up-to-the-minute furnishings money can buy,' he had once teased, when she'd stood staring in rapt fixation at a four-poster bed strewn with a million cushions in the window of a department store. She'd waxed lyrical then about the romance of four-poster beds and had told him, sheepishly, that the family home was anything but modern.

'My mum's like me,' she had confessed with a grin. 'She likes antiques and everything that's old and worn and full of character.'

Javier had personally made sure to insert some pieces of character in the apartment. He, himself, liked modern and minimalist. His impoverished family home had been clean but nearly everything had been bought second-hand. He'd grown up with so many items of furniture that had been just a little too full of character that he was now a fully paid-up member of all things modern and lacking in so-called character.

But he'd enjoyed hand-picking pieces for the apartment, had enjoyed picturing her reaction to the four-poster bed he had bought, the beautifully crafted floral sofa, the thick Persian rug that broke up the expanse of pale flooring.

'The apartment's fine.' Sophie stepped away from

him and folded her arms. 'Better than fine,' she admitted, eyes darting to him and then staying there because he was just so arresting. 'I love the way it's been done. You should congratulate your interior designer.'

'Who said I used one?' He looked at her with raised eyebrows and she blushed in sudden confusion, because to picture him hand-picking anything was somehow... *intimate*. And of course he would never have done any such thing. What über-rich single guy would ever waste time hunting down rugs and curtains? Definitely not a guy like Javier, who was macho to the very last bone in his body.

'I'm afraid there's not a great deal of food.' She turned away because her heart was beating so fast she could barely breathe properly. His presence seemed to infiltrate every part of the apartment, filling it with suffocating, masculine intensity. This was how it had always been with him. In his presence, she'd felt weak and pleasurably helpless. Even as a young guy, struggling to make ends meet, he'd still managed to project an air of absolute assurance. He'd made all the other students around him seem like little boys in comparison.

The big difference was that, back then, she'd had a remit to bask and luxuriate in that powerful masculinity. She could touch, she could run her fingers through his springy, black hair and she'd had permission to melt at the feel of it.

She'd been allowed to want him and to show him how much she wanted him.

Not so now.

Furthermore, she didn't *want* to want him. She didn't

want to feel herself dragged back into a past that was gone for good. Of course, foolish love was gone for good, and no longer a threat to the ivory tower she had constructed around herself that had been so vital in withstanding the years spent with her husband, but she didn't want to feel that pressing, urgent *want* either…

She didn't *want* to feel her heart fluttering like an adolescent's because he happened to be sharing the same space as her. She'd grown up, gone through some hellish stuff. Her outlook on life had been changed for ever because of what she'd had to deal with. She had no illusions now and no longer believed that happiness was her right. It wasn't and never would be. Javier Vasquez belonged to a time when unfettered optimism had been her constant companion. Now, not only was the murky past an unbreachable wall between them, but so were all the changes that had happened to her.

'I wasn't expecting company.' She half turned to find him right behind her, having followed her into the kitchen.

The kitchen was big, a clever mix of old and new, and she felt utterly at home in it.

'Smells good. What is it?'

'Just some tomato sauce. I was going to have it with pasta.'

'You never used to enjoy cooking.' Yet again, he found himself referring to the past, dredging it up and bringing it into the present, where it most certainly did not belong.

'I know.' She shot him a fleeting smile as he sat down at the table, angling his chair so that he could extend his long legs to one side. 'I never had to do it,' she explained. 'Mum loved cooking and I was always happy to let her get on with it. When she got ill, she said it used to occupy her and take her mind off her health problems, so I never interfered. I mean, I'd wash the dishes and tidy behind her, but she liked being the main chef. And then...'

She sighed and began finishing the food preparation, but horribly aware of those lazy, speculative eyes on her, following her every movement.

Javier resisted the urge to try to prise answers out of her. 'So you learned to cook,' he said, moving the conversation along, past the point of his curiosity.

'And discovered that I rather enjoyed it.' She didn't fail to notice how swiftly he had diverted the conversation from the controversial topic of her past, the years she had spent after they had gone their separate ways. His initial curiosity was gone, and she told herself that she was very thankful that it had, because there was far too much she could never, would never, tell him.

But alongside that relief was a certain amount of disappointment, because his lack of curiosity was all wrapped up with the indifference he felt for her.

She suddenly had the strangest temptation to reach out and touch him, to stroke his wrist, feel the familiar strength of his forearm under her fingers. What would he do? How would he react? *Would he recoil with horror or would he touch her back?*

Appalled, she thrust a plate of food in front of him and sat down opposite him. She wanted to sit on her treacherous hands just in case they did something wildly inappropriate of their own accord and she had to remind herself shakily that she was a grown woman, fully in control of her wayward emotions. Emotions that had been stirred up, as they *naturally* would be, by having him invade her life out of the blue.

She heard herself babbling on like the village idiot about her culinary exploits while he ate and listened in silence, with every show of interest in what she was saying.

Which was remarkable, given she had just finished a lengthy anecdote about some slow-cooked beef she had tried to cook weeks previously, which had been disastrous.

'So you like the apartment,' Javier drawled, eyes not leaving her face as he sipped some wine. 'And the job? Now that the work of trying to repair the damage done over the years has begun?'

'It's…awkward,' Sophie told him truthfully.

'Explain.'

'You were right,' she said bluntly, rising to begin clearing the table, her colour high. 'Some of the people my father trusted have let the company down badly over the years. I can only think that employing friends was a luxury my father had when he started the company, and he either continued to trust that they were doing a good job or he knew that they weren't but found it difficult to let them go. And then…'

'And then?' Javier queried silkily and Sophie shrugged.

'Getting rid of them never happened. Thankfully the majority have now left, but with generous pension payments or golden handshakes…' Yet more ways money had drained away from the company until the river had run dry.

'The company is in far worse shape than even I imagined...'

Sophie blanched. She watched as he began helping to clear the table, bringing plates to the sink.

'What do you mean?'

'Your father didn't just take his eye off the ball when he became ill. I doubt his eye had ever really been fully on it in the first place.'

'You can't say that!'

'I've gone through all the books with a fine-tooth comb, Sophie.' He relieved her of the plate she was holding and dried it before placing it on the kitchen counter, then he slung the tea towel he had fetched over his shoulder and propped himself against the counter, arms folded.

Javier had always suspected that her father had been instrumental in her decision to quit university and return to the guy she had always been destined to marry. Even though she had never come right out and said so; even though she had barely had the courage to look him in the face when she had announced that she'd be leaving university because of a family situation that had arisen.

He had never told her that he had subsequently gone to see her parents, that he had confronted her father, who had left him in no doubt that there was no way his precious daughter would contemplate a permanent relationship with someone like him.

He wondered whether the old man's extreme reaction

had been somehow linked to his decline into terminal ill health, and scowled as he remembered the heated argument that had resulted in him walking away, never looking back.

This was the perfect moment to disabuse her of whatever illusions she had harboured about a father who had clearly had little clue about running a business, but the dismay on her face made him hesitate.

He raked his fingers uncomfortably through his hair and continued to stare down at her upturned face.

'He was a terrific dad,' she said defensively, thinking back to the many times he had taken the family out on excursions, often leaving the running of the company to the guys working for him. 'Life was to be enjoyed' had always been his motto. He had played golf and taken them on fantastic holidays; she recognised now that ineffective, relatively unsupervised management had not helped the company coffers. He had inherited a thriving business but, especially when everything had gone electronic, he had failed to move with the times and so had his pals who had joined the company when he had taken it over.

In retrospect, she saw that so much had been piling up like dark clouds on the horizon, waiting for their moment to converge and create the thunderstorm of events that would land her where she was right now.

Javier opened his mouth to disabuse her of her girlish illusions and then thought of his own father. There was no way he would ever have had a word said against him, and yet, hadn't Pedro Vasquez once confessed that he had blown an opportunity to advance himself by storming out of his first company, too young and hot-headed to take orders he didn't agree with? The golden opportunity he had walked away from had never again returned and he had had to devote years of saving and scrimping to get by on the low wages he had earned until his retirement.

But Javier had never held that weak moment against him.

'Your father wouldn't be the first man who failed to spot areas for expansion,' he said gruffly. 'It happens.'

Sophie knew that he had softened and something deep inside her shifted and changed as she continued to stare up at him, their eyes locked.

She could scarcely breathe.

'Thank you,' she whispered and he shook his head, wanting to break a connection that was sucking him in, but finding it impossible to do so.

'What are you thanking me for?'

'He was old-fashioned, and unfortunately the people he delegated to were as old-fashioned as he was. Dad should have called a troubleshooter in the minute the profits started taking a nosedive, but he turned a blind eye to what was going on in the company.'

And he turned a blind eye to your ex as well…

That thought made Javier stiffen. Her father had been old-fashioned enough to hold pompous, arrogant views about *foreign upstarts*, to have assumed that some loser with the right accent was the sort of man his daughter should marry.

But that wasn't a road he was willing to go down because it would have absolved Sophie of guilt and the bottom line was that no one had pointed a gun to her head and forced her up the aisle.

She had *wanted* to take that step.

She had *chosen* to stick with the guy even though she knew that he was blowing up the company with his crazy investments.

She had *watched* and *remained silent* as vast sums of vitally needed money had been gambled away.

She had *enabled*. And the only reason she had done that was because she had loved the man.

He turned away abruptly, breaking eye contact, feeling the sour taste of bile rise to his mouth.

'The company will have to be streamlined further,' he told her curtly. 'Dead wood can no longer be tolerated.' He remained where he was, hip against the counter, and watched as she tidied, washed dishes, dried them and stayed silent.

'All the old retainers will end up being sacked. Is that it?'

'Needs must.'

'Some of the old guys have families… They're nearing retirement—and, okay, they may not have been the most efficient on the planet, but they've been loyal…'

'And you place a lot of value on loyalty, do you?' he murmured.

'Don't you?'

'There are times when common sense has to win the battle.'

'You're in charge now. I don't suppose I have any choice, have I?'

Instead of soothing him, her passive, resentful compliance stoked a surge of anger inside him.

'If you'd taken a step back,' he said with ruthless precision, 'and swapped blind loyalty for some common sense, you might have been able to curb some of your dear husband's outrageous excesses...'

'You truly believe that?' She stepped back, swamped by his powerful, aggressive presence, and glared at him.

The last thing Javier felt he needed was to have her try to make feeble excuses for the man who had contributed to almost destroying her family business. What he really felt he needed right now was something stiff to drink. He couldn't look at her without his body going into instant and immediate overdrive and he couldn't talk to her without relinquishing some of his formidable and prized self-control. She affected him in a way no other woman ever had and it annoyed the hell out of him.

'What else is anyone supposed to believe?' he asked with rampant sarcasm. 'Join the dots and you usually get an accurate picture at the end of the exercise.'

'There was no way I could ever have stopped Roger!' Sophie heard herself all but shout at him, appalled by her outburst even as she realised that it was too late to take it back. 'There were always consequences for trying to talk common sense into him!'

The silence that greeted this outburst was electric, sizzling around them, so that the hairs on the back of her neck stood on end.

'Consequences? What consequences?' Javier pressed in a dangerously soft voice.

'Nothing,' Sophie muttered, turning away, but he reached out, circling her forearm to tug her back towards him.

'You don't get to walk away from this conversation after you've opened up a can of worms, Sophie.'

There were so many reasons this was a can of worms that she didn't want to explore. On a deeply emotional level, she didn't want to confront, yet again, the mistakes she had made in the past. She'd done enough of that to last a lifetime and she especially didn't want to confront those mistakes aloud, with Javier as her witness. She didn't want his pity. She didn't want him to sense her vulnerability. He might no longer care about her, but she didn't want to think that he would be quietly satisfied that, having walked out on him, she had got her comeuppance, so to speak.

'It's not relevant!' she snapped, trying and failing to tug her arm out of his grasp.

'Was he...? I don't know what to think here, Soph...'

That abbreviation of her name brought back a flood of memories and they went straight to the core of her, burning a hole through her defence mechanisms. Her soft mouth trembled and she knew that her eyes were glazing over, which, in turn, made her blink rapidly, fighting back the urge to burst into tears.

'He could be unpredictable.' Her jaw tightened and she looked away but he wouldn't allow her to avoid his searching gaze, tilting her to face him by placing a finger gently under her chin.

'That's a big word. Try breaking it down into smaller components...'

'He could be verbally abusive,' she told him jerkily. 'On one occasion he was physically abusive. So there you have it, Javier. If I'd tried to interfere in his gambling, there's no accounting for what the outcome might have been for me.'

Javier was horrified. He dropped his hand and his fingers clenched and unclenched. She might have fancied herself in love with the guy but that would have been disillusionment on a grand scale.

'Why didn't you divorce him?'

'It was a brief marriage, Javier. And there is more to this than you know...'

'Did you know that the man had anger issues?' Javier sifted his fingers through his hair. Suddenly the kitchen felt the size of a matchbox. He wanted to walk, unfettered; he wanted to punch something.

'Of course I didn't, and that certainly wasn't the case when... You don't get it,' she said uneasily. 'And I'd really rather not talk about this any more.'

Javier had been mildly incredulous at her declaration that her descent into penury had been tougher to handle than his own lifetime of struggle and straitened circumstances. She, at least, had had the head start of the silver spoon in the mouth and a failing company was, after all, still a company with hope of salvation. The crumbling family pile was still a very big roof over her head.

Now there were muddy, swirling currents underlying those glib assumptions, and yet again, he lost sight of the clarity of his intentions.

He reminded himself that fundamentally nothing

had changed. She had begun something seven years ago
and had failed to finish it because she had chosen to run
off with her long-time, socially acceptable boyfriend.

That the boyfriend had failed to live up to expectation, that events in her life had taken a fairly disastrous turn, did not change the basic fact that she had
strung him along.

But he couldn't recapture the simple black-and-white
equation that had originally propelled him. He wondered, in passing, whether he should just have stuck
to his quid pro quo solution: 'you give me what I want
and I'll give you what you want'.

But no.

He wanted so much more and he could feel it running hot through his veins as she continued to stare at
him, unable to break eye contact.

Subtly, the atmosphere shifted. He sensed the change
in her breathing, saw the way her pupils dilated, the
way her lips parted as if she might be on the brink of
saying something.

He cupped her face with his hand and *felt* rather than
heard the long sigh that made her shudder.

Sophie's eyelids felt heavy. She wanted to close her
eyes because if she closed her eyes she would be able
to breathe him in more deeply, and she wanted to do
that, wanted to *breathe him in*, wanted to touch him and
scratch the itch that had been bothering her ever since
he had been catapulted back into her life.

She wanted to kiss him and taste his mouth.

She only realised that she was reaching up to him

when she felt the hardness of muscled chest under the palms of her flattened hands.

She heard a whimper of sheer longing which seemed to come from her and then she was kissing him...tongues entwining...exploring...easing some of the aching pain of her body...

She inched closer, pressed herself against him and wanted to rub against his length, wanted to feel his nakedness against hers.

She couldn't get enough of him.

It was as if no time had gone by between them, as if they were back where they had been, a time when he had been able to set fire to her body with the merest of touches. Nothing had changed and everything had changed.

'No!' She came to her senses with horrified, jerky panic. 'This is... I am *not* that girl I once was. I... *No!*'

She'd flung herself at him! She'd practically assaulted the man like a sex-starved woman desperate to be touched! He didn't even care about her! She'd opened up and on the back of that had leapt on him and had managed to surface only after damage had been done!

Humiliation tore through her. She went beetroot-red and stumbled backwards.

'I apologise for that.' She immediately went on the attack. 'It should never have happened and I don't know what came over me!' She ran her fingers through her hair and tried to remain calm but she was shaking like a leaf. 'This isn't what we're about! Not at all.'

Javier raised his eyebrows and her colour deepened.

'There's only business between us,' she insisted

through clenched teeth. 'I must have had... I don't normally drink...'

'Now, isn't that the lamest excuse in the world?' Javier murmured. 'Let's blame it on the wine...'

'I don't care what you think!' How could he be so *cool and composed* when she was all over the place? Except, of course, she knew how. Because she was just so much more affected by him than he was by her and she could see all her pride and self-respect disappearing down the plug hole if she didn't get a grip on the situation *right now*.

She cleared her throat and stared, at him and through him. 'I... We have to work alongside one another for a while and...this was just an unfortunate blip. I would appreciate it if you never mention it again. We can both pretend that it never happened, because it will never happen again.'

Javier lowered his eyes and tilted his head to one side as if seriously considering what she had just said.

So many challenges in that single sentence. Did she really and truly believe that she could close the book now that page one had been turned?

He'd tasted her and one small taste wasn't going to do. Not for him and not for her. Whatever her backstory, they both needed to sate themselves with one another and that was what they would do before that place was inevitably reached where walking away was an option.

'If that's how you want to play it.' He shrugged and looked at her. 'And from Monday,' he said with lazy assurance, 'bank on me being around most of the time. We both want the same thing, don't we...?'

'What?' Confused, the only thought that came to her was *each other*—that, at any rate, was the thing that *she* wanted, and she could *smell* that it was what he wanted as well.

'For us to sort out the problems in this company as quickly as possible,' he said in a voice implying surprise that she hadn't spotted the right answer immediately. 'Of course…'

CHAPTER SIX

'No.'

'Give me three good reasons and maybe I'll let you get away with that response.'

Sophie stared at Javier, body language saying it all as she supported herself on her desk, palms flattened on the highly polished surface, torso tilted towards him in angry refusal.

True to his word, he had more or less taken up residence in the premises in Notting Hill.

He wasn't there *all* the time. That would actually have been far easier for her to deal with. No, he breezed in and out. Sometimes she would arrive at eight-thirty to find him installed at the desk which he had claimed as his own, hard at it, there since the break of dawn and with a list of demands that had her on her feet running at full tilt for the remainder of the day.

Other times he might show up mid-afternoon and content himself with checking a couple of things with members of staff before vanishing, barely giving her a second glance.

And there had been days when he hadn't shown up at all and there had been no communication from him.

After six weeks, Sophie felt as though she had been tossed in a tumble dryer with the speed turned to high. She had been miserable, uncertain and fearful when she had had to deal with the horrendous financial mess into which she had been plunged. After her marriage, that had just felt like a continuation of a state of mind that had become more or less natural to her.

Now, though…

She was none of those things. She was a high-wire walker, with excitement and trepidation fighting for dominance. She leapt out of bed every morning with a treacherous sense of anticipation. Her pulses raced every time she took a deep breath and entered the office. Her blood pressure soared when she glanced to the door and saw him stride in. Her heart sang when she saw him stationed at his desk first thing, with his cup of already tepid black coffee on the desk in front of him.

Life was suddenly in technicolor and it scared the living daylights out of her. It had become obvious that she'd never got him out of her system and she seemed to have no immunity against the staggering force of his impact on all her senses. Her heart might be locked away behind walls of ice but her body clearly wasn't.

'I don't have to give you any reasons, Javier.' She was the last man standing and had been about to leave the office at a little after six when Javier had swanned in and stopped her in the act of putting on her jacket.

'Quick word,' he had said, in that way he had of presuming that there would be no argument. He'd then proceeded to lounge back in his chair, gesturing for her to drop what she was doing and take the seat facing him across his desk.

That had been half an hour ago.

'You do, really.' He looked at her lazily. Despite the fact that the largely young staff all dressed informally, Sophie had stuck it out with her prissy work outfits, which ranged from drab grey skirts and neat white blouses to drab black skirts and neat white blouses, all worn with the same flat black pumps. The ravishing hair which he had glimpsed on the one occasion when he had surprised her weeks ago at the apartment had gone back into hiding. Woe betide she actually released it from captivity between the hours of eight-thirty and five-thirty!

'Why?'

'Because I think it would work.'

'And of course, because *you* think it would work, means *I* have to agree and go along with it!'

'How many of the programmes that I've set in motion over the past couple of months have failed?'

'That's not the point.'

'Any? No. Is the company seeing the start of a turn-around? Yes. Have the sales team been reporting gains? Yes.' He folded his hands behind his head and looked at her evenly. 'Ergo, this idea makes sense and will generate valuable sales.'

'But I'm not a model, Javier!'

'That's the point, Sophie. You're the face of your company. Putting your image on billboards and in advertising campaigns will personalise the company—half the battle in wooing potential customers is making them feel as though they're relating to something more than just a name and a brand.'

She stared at him mutinously and he gazed calmly back at her.

The waiting game was taking longer than he had anticipated and he was finding that he was in no rush to speed things up. He was enjoying her. He was enjoying the way she made him feel and it wasn't just the reaction of his body to her. No, he realised that the years of having whatever he wanted and whoever he chose had jaded him. This blast from the past was…*rejuvenating*. And who didn't like a spot of rejuvenation in their lives? Of course, he would have to hurry things along eventually, because bed was the conclusion to the exercise before normal service was resumed and he returned to the life from which he had been taking a little holiday.

But for the moment…

He really liked the way she blushed. He could almost forget that she was the scheming young girl who had played him for an idiot.

'So we just need to talk about the details. And stop glaring. I thought all women liked to show off their bodies.'

Sophie glared. 'Really, Javier? You really think that?'

'Who wouldn't like to be asked to model?'

'Is that the message you've got from…from the women you've been out with?'

Javier looked at her narrowly because this was the first time she had ventured near the question of his love life. 'Most of the women I've been out with,' he murmured, 'were already catwalk models, accustomed to dealing with the full glare of the public spotlight.'

She'd wondered. Of course she had. Now she knew. Models. Naturally. He certainly wouldn't have dated normal, average women holding down normal, average jobs. He was the man who could have it all and men who could have it all always, but always, seemed to want to have models glued to their arm. It was just so...*predictable*.

'You've stopped glaring,' Javier said. 'Which is a good thing. But now there's disapproval stamped all over your face. What are you disapproving of? My choice of woman?'

'I don't care what your choice of girlfriends has been!'

'Don't you?' He raised his eyebrows. 'Because you look a little agitated. What's wrong with models? Some of them can be relatively clever, as it happens.'

'Relatively clever...' Sophie snorted. Her colour was high and the look in his sinfully dark eyes was doing weird things to her, making her feel jumpy and thrillingly excited.

Making her nipples tighten...stoking a dampness between her thighs that had nothing to do with her scorn for his choice of dates, whoever those nameless dates had been.

Instant recall of that kiss they had shared made her breath hitch temporarily in her throat.

Just as she had stridently demanded, no mention had been made of it again. It was as though it had never happened. Yes, that was exactly what she had wanted, but it hadn't stopped her constantly harking back to it in her head, reliving the moment and burning up just at the thought of it. How could a bruised and battered heart take second billing to a body that seemed to do whatever it felt like doing?

'You used to tell me that you liked the fact that I had opinions!'

'Many models have opinions—admittedly not of the intellectual variety. They have very strong opinions on, oh, shoes…bags…other models…'

Sophie felt her mouth twitch. She'd missed his sense of humour. In fact, thinking about it, he'd been the benchmark against which Roger had never stood a chance. Not that he had ever been in the running…

In fact, thinking about it, wasn't he the benchmark against which every other man had always been set and always would be? When would that end? How could she resign herself to a half-life because she was still wrapped up in the man in front of her? Because that intense physical reaction just hadn't died and could still make itself felt through all the layers of sadness and despair that had shaped the woman she was now.

She hadn't looked twice at any guy since she'd been on her own. Hadn't even been tempted!

Yet here she was, not only wanting to look but wanting to touch…

Why kid herself? Telling herself to pretend that that kiss had never happened didn't actually mean that it had disappeared from her head.

And telling herself that she should feel nothing for a guy who belonged to her past, a guy who wasn't even interested in her, didn't actually mean that she felt nothing for him.

Lust—that was what it was—and the harder she tried to deny its existence, the more powerful a grip it seemed to have over her.

And part of the reason was because…he *wasn't* indifferent, was he?

Heart racing, she looked down and gave proper house room in her head to all those barely discernible signals she had felt emanating from him over the past few weeks.

For starters, there had been *that kiss*.

She'd felt the way his mouth had explored hers, hungry and greedy and wanting more.

And then, working in the same space, she'd lodged somewhere in the back of her head those accidental brushes when he had leant over her, caging her in in front of her computer so that he could explain some detail on the screen.

She'd committed to memory the way she had occasionally surprised his lazy dark eyes resting on her just a fraction longer than necessary.

And sometimes…didn't he stand just a little too close? Close enough for her to feel the heat from his body? To smell his clean, masculine scent?

Didn't all of that add up to something?

She didn't know whether he was even aware of the dangerous current running between them just beneath the surface. If he was, then it was obvious that he had no intention of doing anything about it.

And then, one day, he would no longer be around.

Right now, he was making sure that his investment paid off. He had sunk money into a bailout, and he wasn't going to see that money flushed down the drain, so he was taking an active part in progressing the company.

But soon enough the company would be on firmer ground and he would be able to retreat and hand over the running of it to other people, herself included.

He would resume his hectic life running his own empire.

And she, likewise, would return to Yorkshire to take up full-time residence in the family home, which she would be able to renovate at least enough to make it a viable selling proposition.

They would part company.

And she would be left with this strange, empty feeling for the rest of her life.

She felt guilty enough about the way they had broken up. On top of that, he would remain the benchmark against which no other man would ever stand a chance of competing for ever.

She should have slept with him.

She knew that now. She should have slept with him instead of holding on to all those girlish fantasies about saving herself for when that time came and she knew that they would be a permanent item, for when she was convinced that their relationship was made to stand the test of time.

If she'd slept with him, he would never have achieved the impossible status of being the only guy capable of turning her on. If she'd slept with him, she might not feel so guilty about the way everything had crashed and burned.

Was it selfish now to think that, if she righted that oversight, she might be free to get on with her life? Things were being sorted financially but what was the good of that if, emotionally, she remained in some kind of dreadful, self-inflicted limbo?

She wasn't the selfish sort. She had never thought of herself as the kind of pushy, independent type who took what she wanted from a man to satisfy her own needs.

The opposite!

But she knew, with a certain amount of desperation, that if she didn't take what she wanted now she would create all sorts of problems for herself down the line.

She wondered whether she could talk to her mother about it and immediately dismissed that thought because, as far as Evelyn Griffin-Watt was concerned, Javier was a youthful blip who had been cut out of her life a long time ago, leaving no nasty scars behind.

Besides, her mother was leading an uncomplicated and contented life in Cornwall; was it really fair to bring back unpleasant memories by resurrecting a long, involved conversation about the past?

'Okay.'

'Come again?'

'I'll do it.'

Javier smiled slowly. In truth, the whole modelling idea had sprung to mind only the day before, and he had anticipated defeat, but here she was…agreeing after a pretty half-hearted battle. At least, half-hearted for her.

'Brilliant decision!'

'I was railroaded into it.'

'Strong word. I prefer *persuaded*. Now, I have a few ideas…'

Sophie peeped through a crack in the curtains and looked down into the courtyard which had been tarted up for the day into a vision of genteel respectability.

The shoot had been arranged in the space of a week, during which time Sophie had spoken to various media types and also to various stylists. She imagined that they were being paid a phenomenal amount for the day because they had all bent over backwards to pay attention to what she had said.

Which hadn't been very much because she had no idea what questions to ask other than the obvious one: *How long is it all going to take?*

Javier hadn't been at any of those meetings, choosing instead to delegate to one of the people in his PR department, but that hadn't bothered Sophie.

In a way, she'd been glad, because she had a plan and the element of surprise was a big part of the plan.

Except, the day had now arrived and the courtyard was buzzing with cameramen, the make-up crew, the director, producer and all the other people whose roles were, quite frankly, bewildering. And where was Javier? Nowhere to be seen.

It was today or it was not at all.

She dropped the curtain and turned to the full-length mirror which the stylist had installed in the bedroom because the small one on the dressing table *'just won't do, darling!'*

The brief which she had agreed on with Javier would have her standing next to a gleaming articulated lorry bearing the company logo, in dungarees, a checked shirt and a jaunty cowboy hat on her head.

Sophie had decided to take it up a notch and the reflection staring back at her had dumped the dungarees in favour of a pair of shorts with a frayed hem. The checked shirt remained the same, but it was tied under her breasts so that her flat stomach was exposed, and there was no jaunty cowboy hat on her head. Instead, she had slung it on her back so that her hair was wild and loose.

Javier had vaguely aimed for something wholesome and appealing, a throwback to the good old days of home-baked bread and jam, which was some of the cargo transported in the lorries. He'd suggested that it would be a nice contrast to the new face of the business, which was streamlined and fully up to spec on the technological front, which it hadn't been before. Something along the lines of the home-baked bread getting from A to B before it had time to cool from the oven and Sophie's image was going to sell the absolute truth of that.

She had taken it up a notch from wholesome to wholesome *and sexy*.

It had been her brainwave when she had sat there, numbly recognising that she would never, ever get over him if she didn't sleep with him, if she didn't seduce him into bed. He'd been in her head for years and she couldn't think of another way to make sure that he was knocked off the position he occupied there.

She'd never seduced anyone in her life before. Just thinking about doing something like that was terrifying, but when it came to her emotions, she had to be proactive. As proactive as she had been dealing with the mess she'd been left to clear up in the company.

She wasn't a simpering teenager any more, seeing the future through rose-tinted specs and believing in happy-ever-after endings.

She was an adult, jaded by experience, who would be left nursing regret for the rest of her life if she didn't give this a shot. And so what if she failed? What if he looked at her get-up and burst out laughing? So, she might have a moment's humiliation, but that would be worth the lifetime she would have had thinking about an opportunity that had passed her by, an opportunity to claim what she knew could have been hers all those years ago.

The time had come to take a chance.

Except, it didn't look as though the wretched man was going to show up!

Her nerves were shot, her pulses were racing and she hadn't eaten since lunchtime the previous day because of the shot nerves and the racing pulses...

She was a mess and it was all going to be for nothing because Javier had obviously had his brainwave and then allowed his minions to realise it while he stepped back from the scene of the action.

She slunk down to the courtyard with a white bathrobe over her screamingly uncomfortable outfit and was immediately appropriated by a host of people whose only function seemed to be to get her ready for *the shoot*.

She allowed herself to be manoeuvred while disappointment cascaded through her in waves.

No Javier. No big seduction. It had taken absolutely everything out of her. And there was no way she was going to do this again. She wasn't going to set herself the task of staging seductive scenes in the hope of igniting something that probably wasn't there for him anyway, whatever stupid signals she thought she'd read!

A mirror was brought for her to inspect herself. Sophie barely glanced at the fully made-up face staring back at her. After the tension of the past couple of days, and the nervous excitement of earlier this morning as she had got dressed, she now felt like a balloon that had been deflated before it had made it to the party.

She was aware of orders being shouted and poses she was being instructed to adopt.

No one had questioned the slight change in outfit. She was Javier's personal pet project and no one dared question her for fear that she would report unfavourably back to their boss.

She was supposed to turn up in denim and a checked top with a cowboy hat and they knew what the direction of the shoot should be. The outfit was daring, though, and the poses were therefore slightly more daring than perhaps originally choreographed.

She had her back to the camera team, one hand resting lightly on the shining lorry, looking over her shoulder with a smile, when she heard his roar from behind her.

She'd given up on Javier coming.

But before she'd clocked his absence, she had somehow imagined him standing amongst the crew, goggle-eyed as he looked at her, wanting her as much as she wanted him and knowing that he had to have her. She'd pictured him waiting impatiently until the crew had packed up and gone and then…

Her wanton thoughts had not formulated much beyond that point. There would be a lot of ground to cover before the scene shifted from impatient seduction to the satisfied aftermath.

'What the hell is going on here?'

Sophie stumbled back against the lorry and the entire assembled crew stared at Javier in growing confusion, aware that they had done something wrong but not quite sure what.

Javier strode forward through them like a charging bull, face as black as thunder.

'You!' He pointed to the director of the shoot, who jumped to attention and began stammering out his consternation, puzzled as to what the problem was. The shoot was going very well. Indeed, if Javier wanted, he could see what was already in the bag. It was going to do the job and sell the business like hot cakes straight from the oven. Sophie was a brilliant model. No temper tantrums and no diva pouting. She was perfect for the job and the fact that she was part-owner of the company was going to be a nice touch. They'd make sure they got that in in the backdrop…

Javier held up one cold, imperious hand. 'This was not what I wanted!' he snapped. He looked across to Sophie with a scowl and she folded her arms defensively.

'They have no idea what you're going on about, Javier,' she said sweetly, strolling towards him although she was quaking inside, unable to tear her eyes away from his strident masculinity. He dominated the space around him, a towering, forbidding figure who clearly inspired awe, fear and respect in equal measure.

It was an incredible turn-on to think that this was the guy who had once teased her, told her that she made him weak, the guy whose eyes had flared with desire whenever they had rested on her.

The guy she wanted so much that it hurt.

The guy she was prepared to risk humiliation for.

'Consider this shoot over for the day.' He directed the command at the director but his eyes were focused on Sophie as she moved to stand right in front of him.

He cursed the overseas phone call that had held him up and then the traffic on the motorways and B-roads that wound their way to her family home. If he'd arrived when he had originally planned, he would have…

Made sure that she didn't step one delicate foot out of the house dressed in next to nothing.

He was shocked by his sudden regression to a Neanderthal, which was the very opposite of the cool composure he prided himself on having.

Hands thrust deep into his pockets, he continued to stare at her with ferocious intent while the entire assembled crew hurriedly began packing their equipment and disappearing fast.

Sophie heard the gravelly chaos of reversing cars and SUVs but she was locked into a little bubble in which the only two people who existed were herself and Javier.

'That wasn't the outfit we agreed on.' His voice was a low, driven snarl and she tilted her chin at a mutinous angle.

'Checked shirt…*tick*. Denim…*tick*. Stupid cowboy hat…*tick*. Trainers…*tick*…'

'You know what I mean,' Javier gritted, unable to take his eyes off her.

'Do I?' She hadn't realised how chilly it was and she hugged herself.

'You're cold,' he said gruffly, removing his jacket and settling it around her shoulders. For a second, she just wanted to close her eyes and breathe in the scent from it.

And this was what it was all about. This *hunger* that had never gone away, but which *had* to go away, because if it didn't it would eat away at her for ever. And there was only one way of it just *going away and leaving her alone*.

'Tell me,' she pressed huskily. 'Why are you so furious? It wasn't fair of you to send all those poor people packing. They were only doing their job.'

'That's not the way I see it,' Javier growled. The jacket, way too big, drowned her and it was really weird the way that just made her look even sexier. He shifted in an attempt to ease the discomfort of his erection. Was she wearing a bra? He didn't think so and that made him angry all over again.

'How do you see it?'

'The brief was for you to look wholesome!' He raked his fingers through his hair and shook his head. This was the first time he had ventured to her family home but he hadn't noticed a single brick. His entire focus was on her. She consumed him. 'The attractive girl next door! Not a sex siren out to snag a man! How the hell is *that* supposed to sell the company?'

'I thought that sex sold everything?'

'Is that why you did it? Was that your concept of positive input? Dressing up in next to nothing and draping yourself over that lorry like a hooker posing in a motorbike shot?'

'How *dare you*?' But she flushed and cringed and knew that there was some justification for that horrible slur. She barely stopped to think that in summer there were many, many girls her age who went out dressed like this and thought nothing of it. She just knew that it wasn't *her*.

'The entire crew,' he delineated coldly, 'must have had a field day ogling you. Or maybe that was what you had in mind. Is that it? Has living in London kick-started an urge to push the limits? Have you realised how much tamer your life up here was?'

'I didn't do this so that any of the crew could *ogle me*.' She fought to maintain his cool, disapproving stare and took a deep breath. 'I did this so that...' Her voice faltered. Her hands were clammy and she licked her lips as the tension stretched and stretched between them.

'So that...?' Javier prompted softly.

'So that *you* could ogle me...'

CHAPTER SEVEN

THIS WAS WHAT he had been waiting for, the slow burn until the conflagration, because he knew that it would be a conflagration. She oozed sex appeal without even realising it. And she had come to him. He hadn't been mistaken about those invisible signals his antennae had been picking up and he marvelled that he had ever doubted himself.

Of course, he would have to make it clear to her that this wasn't some kind of romance, that whatever they did would be a purely physical animal act. They'd had their window for romance once and she'd put paid to that. Romance was definitely off the cards now.

He smiled slowly, his beautiful, sensuous mouth curving as he lazily ran his eyes over her flushed face, taking in everything from the slight tremor of her hands to the nervous tic in her neck, a beating pulse that was advertising what she wanted as loud and as clear as if it had been written in neon lettering over her head.

Him.

She wanted him.

The wheel had turned full circle, and having walked away from him, she was now walking back.

That tasted good and it would taste even better when he laid down his conditions.

'Is that so?' he breathed huskily, his erection threatening to hamper movement.

Sophie didn't say anything in response to that. She read the satisfaction in his gleaming eyes and a primal lust that was so powerful that it easily swept aside any nagging doubt that she might be embarking on the wrong course of action.

He caught the lapels of his jacket and drew her a few inches towards him. 'There were less complicated ways of getting my attention, Soph...' he murmured. 'A simple *I want you* would have done the trick.'

The fact that he made no attempt to kiss her or touch her acted as an unbearably powerful aphrodisiac. Her heart was beating so fast that it felt as though it was going to explode and she was melting everywhere. She licked her lips and Javier followed that tiny movement with such intense concentration that it made her blood heat up even further.

'That would have been...too much,' she breathed. 'It was tough enough...' She gestured down to her lack of outfit and Javier half-smiled, remembering how shy she had once been, despite the fact that she had the face and figure that could turn heads from a mile away.

'Getting into your skimpy little get-up? Let's go inside. It's getting breezier out here.' He kept his distance but the electricity crackled between them. He wasn't touching her and he hardly dared because one touch and he would have to have her at once, fast and hard, up against a wall.

He didn't want that. He wanted slow and leisurely. He wanted to explore every inch of the woman who had escaped him. Only then would he be able to walk away satisfied.

Walking towards the house, he really noticed the signs of disrepair which he had failed to see when he had arrived earlier. He paused and looked critically at the façade and Sophie followed the leisurely and critical inspection, marvelling at the damage that had been done over a handful of years.

She longed to reach out and touch him. She longed to link her fingers through his in the same careless gesture of ownership to which she had once been privy. She reminded herself that times had changed since then. This was something quite, quite different.

'You're right,' Javier said drily, stepping back as she pushed open the front door. 'The place is falling down.'

'I know.' Sophie looked around her, seeing it through his eyes. He was now used to the best that money could buy. The apartment loaned to her was pristine, like something from the centre pages of a house magazine. This house, on the other hand...

They were in a cavernous hall. Javier could see that this would have been an enormous and elegant country estate once upon a time but the paint was peeling, the once ornate ceiling was cracked and he was sure that further exploration would reveal a lot more problems.

'I'm sorry,' he said gravely and Sophie looked at him, startled.

'What for?'

'You told me that penury was harder for you than it ever had been for me and you were probably right. I knew no better and things could only go up. You knew better and the journey down must have been swift and painful. But...' he tilted his head to one side and looked at her '...you coped.'

'I didn't have a choice, did I?' She suddenly felt shy. Should they be heading up to the bedroom? What was the etiquette for two people who had decided that they are going to sleep together? Not in the 'clutching one another while stumbling up the stairs' kind of way, but in the manner of a business transaction. At least that was what it felt like—two people putting an end to their unfinished business.

They wanted each other but neither of them liked it.

'Show me the rest of the place.'

'Why?' She was genuinely puzzled.

'I used to wonder what it was like. You talked about your home a lot when we were...going out. At the time, it had sounded like a slice of paradise, especially compared to where I had grown up.'

'And I bet you're thinking, *how the mighty have fallen...*' She laughed self-consciously because all of a sudden she was walking on quicksand. This was the man she had fallen in love with—a man who was interested, warm, curious, empathetic... For a minute, the cynical, mocking stranger was gone and she was floundering.

'No. I'm not,' he said quietly. 'I'm thinking that it

must have taken a lot of courage not to have cracked under the strain.'

Sophie blushed and began showing him through the various rooms on the ground floor of the house. There were a lot of them and most of them were now closed with the heating off so that money could be saved. When she and Oliver had realised the necessity of putting the house on the market, they had made an effort to do a patch-up job here and there, but not even those dabs of paint in some of the rooms could conceal the disintegrating façade.

The more she talked, the more aware she was of him there by her side, taking it all in. If this was his idea of foreplay, it couldn't have been more effective, because she was on fire.

Talking…who would have thought that it could have changed the atmosphere between them so thoroughly?

Her nipples were tight and tingling and the ache between her thighs made her want to moan out loud. She could *feel* him, could feel herself warming to him, and she had to fight the seductive urge to start mingling the past with the present, confusing the powerful, ruthless man he had become with the man she had once known.

When they were through with the ground floor, she gazed up the sweeping staircase before turning to him and clearing her throat.

'The bedrooms are upstairs.' She wanted to sound controlled and adult, a woman in charge of a situation she had engendered. Instead, she heard the nervous falsetto of her voice and inwardly cringed.

Javier lounged against the door frame, hoping that

it wouldn't collapse under his weight from dry rot or termites. He folded his arms and looked at her as she fidgeted for a few seconds before meeting his gaze.

'Why are you so nervous?' he enquired, reaching out to adjust the collar of the jacket which she was still clutching around her, and then allowing his hands to remain there, resting lightly on her. 'It's not as though you haven't felt the touch of my lips on yours before…'

Sophie inhaled sharply.

She had got this far and now realised that she hadn't actually worked out what happened next. Yes, on the physical level, terrifying and exciting though that was, her body would simply just take over. She knew it would. She remembered what it had felt like to be touched by him, the way he had made her whole body ignite in a burst of red-hot flame.

How much more glorious would it feel to actually *make love* with him…?

She was nervous, yes, thrillingly so at the prospect of making love with him. But there were other things… things that needed to be discussed…and now that the time had come she wondered whether she would be able to open up to him.

'I'm…I'm not nervous about…about…'

'Going to bed with me? Being touched all over by me? Your breasts and nipples with my tongue? Your belly…?' He loved the fluttering of her eyes as she listened, the way her tongue darted out to moisten her lips and the way she was breathing just a little faster; tiny, jerky breaths that were an unbelievable turn-on because they showed him what she was feeling. He doubted that she could even put into words what she was feeling because...

Because of her inherent shyness. It almost made him burst out laughing because she was far from shy. She was a widow who had been through the mill.

'I'm not nervous about any of that!' Sophie glared at him. 'Not really.'

'You're as jumpy as a cat on a hot tin roof, Sophie. If that's not nerves, then I don't know what is.'

'I need to talk to you,' she said jerkily and watched as the shutters instantly came down over his beautiful eyes.

'Is this the part where you start backtracking?' he asked softly. 'Because I don't like those sorts of games. You did a runner on me once before and I wouldn't like to think that I'm in line for a repeat performance...'

Sophie chewed her lip nervously. To open up would expose so much and yet how could she not?

How else would she be able to explain away the fact that she was still a virgin?

A virgin widow. It wasn't the first time that she'd wanted to laugh at the irony of that. Laugh or cry. Maybe both.

Would he even notice that she was a virgin? He would know that she lacked experience but would he really notice just how inexperienced she truly was?

Could she pretend?

'I'm not backtracking.' She glanced up the stairs and then began heading up, glancing over her shoulder just once. At the top of the staircase, she eased the jacket off and slung it over the banister. 'If I didn't want to do this…' she half-smiled '…would I be doing *this*?'

Javier looked at her long and hard and then returned that half-smile with one of his own.

'No, I don't suppose you would be,' he murmured, taking the steps two at a time until he was right by her, crowding her in a way that was very, very sexy.

He curved his big hand behind the nape of her neck and kissed her.

With a helpless whimper, Sophie leant into him. She undid a couple of his shirt buttons and slipped her hands underneath the silky cotton and the helpless whimper turned into a giddy groan as she felt the hard muscle of his chest.

This was what she had dreamed of and it was only now, when she was touching him, that she realised just how long those dreams had been in her head, never-ending versions of the same thing…*touching him*.

Javier eventually pulled back and gazed down at her flushed face.

'We need to get to a bed.' He barely recognised his own voice, which was thick with desire, the voice of someone drunk with *want*. 'If we don't, I'm going to turn into a caveman, rip off your clothes right here on the staircase and take you before we can make it to a bedroom…'

Sophie discovered that she was wantonly turned on by the image of him doing that.

'My bedroom's just along the corridor,' she whispered huskily, galvanising her jelly-like legs forward.

There were numerous bedrooms on the landing and

most of the doors were shut, which led Javier to assume that they were never used. Probably in as much of a state of disrepair as some of the rooms downstairs which had been sealed off.

Her bedroom was at the very end of the long, wide corridor and it was huge.

'I keep meaning to brighten it up a bit,' she apologised, nervous all over again because, now that they were in the bedroom, all her fears and worries had returned with a vengeance. 'I've had some of the pictures on the walls since I was a kid and now, in a weird way, I would feel quite sad to take them down and chuck them in the bin…'

He was strolling through the bedroom, taking in absolutely everything, from the books on the bookshelf by the window to the little framed family shots in silver frames which were lined up on her dressing table.

Eventually he turned to face her and began unbuttoning his shirt.

Sophie tensed and gulped. She watched in fascination as his shirt fell open, revealing the hard chest she had earlier felt under her fingers.

He shrugged it off and tossed it on the ground and her mouth went dry as he walked slowly towards her.

'There's…there's something I should tell you…' she stammered, frozen to the spot and very much aware of the great big bed just behind her.

Javier didn't break stride.

Talk? He didn't think so. The marriage she had hoped for and the guy she had ditched him to be with hadn't gone according to plan. That changed nothing.

She still remained the same woman who had strung him along and then walked away because, when you got right down to it, he had not been good enough for her.

'No conversation,' he murmured, trailing his finger along her collarbone until she sighed and squirmed and her eyelids fluttered.

'What do you mean?'

'No confidences, no long explanations about why you're doing what you're doing. We both know the reason that we're here.' He hooked his fingers under the checked shirt and circled her waist, then gently began to undo the buttons on the shirt. 'We still want one another,' he murmured, nibbling her ear.

'Yes…' Sophie could barely get the word out. Her body tingled everywhere and his delicate touch sent vibrations racing through her. She rubbed her thighs together and heard him laugh softly, as if he knew that she was trying to ease the pain between them.

'This is all there is, Soph.' There was a finality to stating the obvious which, for some reason, set his teeth on edge, although he didn't quite understand why when it was pretty straightforward a situation. He was propelling her very gently towards the bed; she realised that only when she tumbled back, and then he leant forward, propping himself up on either side of her, staring down at her gravely.

Sophie couldn't have uttered a word if she'd tried. She was mesmerised by the compelling intensity of his expression, the soft, sexy drawl of his voice, the penetrating, opaque blackness of his eyes.

Somehow he had managed to undo every last button

of her shirt and the cool air was a sweet antidote to the heat that was consuming her.

He stood up and paused for a few seconds with his fingers resting loosely on the zipper of his trousers.

She could see the bulge of his erection and half closed her eyes when she thought about the mechanics of something so impressively large entering her.

But no talking, he'd said…

No talking because he wasn't interested in what she had to say.

As though reading the anxious direction of her thoughts, he dropped his hand and joined her on the bed, manoeuvring her onto her side so that they were lying stomach to stomach, then she flopped over onto her back and stared up at the ceiling.

'Look at me, Soph.' He framed her face with his hand so that she was forced to look at him. His breath was warm on her cheek and she wanted to evade the deadly seriousness of his gaze. 'Whatever it is you want to tell me, resist, because I'm not interested.' He felt a sharp jab of pain deep inside him but pressed on, because this had to be said, and wasn't this all part of that wheel turning full circle? That she'd come to him and now, with her in the palm of his hand, he could reduce her to humility? That he could let her know, without even having to vocalise the obvious, that the shoe was firmly on the other foot?

That he was the one calling the shots?

He had the uncomfortable feeling that it should have felt more satisfying than it did.

'This is something we both have to do, wouldn't

you agree? If you hadn't ended up back in my life in a way neither of us could ever have predicted, well, we wouldn't be here now. But we're here and…' He smoothed his hand over her thigh and felt her shudder, wishing she wasn't wearing clothes because he was itching to feel all of her, naked, supple and compliant. 'We have to finish this. But finishing it doesn't involve tender sharing of our life histories. This isn't a courtship and it's important for you to recognise that.'

Sophie felt the hot crawl of colour seep into her cheeks. Of course, he was just being honest. Of course, this was just about the sex they should have had all those years ago. Nothing more. If she could, she would have slid off the bed, looked at him with haughty disdain and told him to clear off, but what her body wanted and *needed* was calling the shots now.

'I know that,' she assured him in a calm voice which was not at all how she was feeling inside. 'I'm not on the lookout for a courtship! Do you really think that I'm the same idiotic young girl you knew all those years ago, Javier? I've grown up! Life has…flattened me in ways you couldn't begin to understand.' Right now, she didn't feel very grown up. Indeed, she felt as unsure and uncertain as a teenager.

But she really wasn't the same girl she had once been. That much, at least, was true.

Javier frowned. Her words were the words of a cynic altered by circumstance, but the tenor of her voice… the soft tremble of her mouth…seemed to be saying something different, which was, of course, ridiculous.

'Good,' he purred. 'So we understand one another.'

'A one-night stand,' she murmured, flattening her hand against his chest as a tingle of unbridled excitement rippled through her. She'd never been a one-night stand kind of girl but a one-night stand with this man would be worth the final demolishing of all her girlhood, or whatever remnants remained in some dark closet at the very back of her mind.

Javier was a little piqued at the speed with which she had accepted the brevity of what they were about to embark on but he was done with thinking.

His erection was so rock-hard it was painful and he took her hand and guided it to his trousers.

'If you don't hold me hard,' he muttered, 'I'm not going to be able to finish what's been started the way it should be finished.'

'What do you mean?'

'I mean it's time to stop talking.'

He stood up in one fluid movement and began undressing. She marvelled at his utter lack of self-consciousness. He looked at her and held her fascinated gaze as he removed his trousers, tossing it on the ground, where it joined his shirt, leaving him in his low-slung silk boxers, which did nothing to conceal the evidence of his arousal.

She did this to him!

Hard on the heels of that thought came another, less welcome one.

How many other women had done this to him? How many women had lain on a bed and watched him with the same open-mouthed fascination with which *she* was now watching him?

He wouldn't have slept with any of *them* because they had started something years ago that needed *to be finished*. He wouldn't have slept with any of them because he'd been *driven to*. He would have slept with them *because he'd wanted to*. The difference felt huge but it was good that she was aware of that, because it would make it easy to walk away when they were finished making love.

It would make it easy to detach.

'I'm really surprised you never got married,' she blurted out and he grinned and slipped onto the bed alongside her.

His erection butted against her thigh and then against her stomach as he angled her to face him.

Javier was accustomed to women who couldn't wait to strip off so that they could show him what was on offer and it was weirdly erotic to be naked and in bed with a woman who was still fully clothed. He couldn't wait to get those clothes off, yet he was reluctant to undress her, wanting to savour the thrill of anticipation.

Once they'd made love, once he'd had her, it would signal the end and where was the harm in delaying that inevitable moment? They had the night to make love and in the morning, with that itch put to rest for ever, he would leave and contrive never to see her again. His relationship with her company would revert to being just another business deal, which would, he knew, be as successful as all the other business deals he had made over the years.

This didn't taste of revenge, not the revenge that he

had seen as his when her brother had first entered his office on a begging mission.

This was a conclusion and it was one over which he had complete control.

He was exactly where he was meant to be and it felt good.

'I don't think marriage and I would make happy bed partners.' He propped himself up on one elbow and began undressing her. 'A successful marriage…' the shirt was off '…requires just the sort of commitment…'

Now she was wriggling out of the shorts, leaving just a pair of lacy briefs that matched her bra. Her breasts were full and firm and he could see the dark circle of her nipples through the lace.

'That I don't have…' He breathed unsteadily. 'Your breasts are driving me crazy, Sophie…' He bent to circle one nipple through the lacy bra with his mouth and she gasped and arched into his questing mouth.

They hadn't even got this far first time round. She had been as prim and as chaste as a Victorian maiden and he had held off, curbing his natural instinct to swoop and conquer. He closed his mind off to the reasons why she had been so damned prim and chaste because the only thing that mattered now was the taste of her.

He didn't unhook the bra. Instead, he pushed it over her breasts and, for a few unbelievably erotic seconds, he just stared. The big, circular discs of her nipples pouted at him. Her breasts were smooth, creamy and soft. He was a teenager again, with a teenager's crazy, wildly out-of-control hormones, trying hard not to come prematurely.

He almost wanted to laugh in disbelief at the extraordinary reaction of his normally well-behaved body.

He licked the stiffened bud of one nipple and then lost himself in something he had dreamed of, suckling and drawing her nipple into his mouth, flicking his tongue over the tip and just loving her responsive body underneath him.

Without breaking the devastating caress, he slid his hand under the small of her back so that she was arched up, writhing and squirming as he moved from nipple to the soft underside of her breast, nuzzling and tasting.

Driving himself mad.

He had to hold off for a few seconds to catch his breath; he had to grit his teeth and summon up all his willpower to withstand the urge of her hand as she reached up, blindly curving the contour of his cheek, desperate for him to resume what he had been doing.

Without his usual finesse, he clumsily ripped the remainder of her clothes off.

How long had he been waiting for this moment? It felt like for ever as he gazed down at her rosy, flushed body, his breathing laboured as if he had just completed a marathon.

She was perfect.

Her skin was silky smooth, her breasts pert, inviting all sorts of wicked thoughts, and as his eyes drifted lower…

The soft, downy hair between her legs elicited a groan that sounded decidedly helpless.

So this was what it felt like…

This heady sense of power as she watched him watching her and losing control.

By the time she had married Roger, she had known the full scale of the mistake she had made, but she had still been young and naïve enough fundamentally to trust that the lectures from her parents about the follies of youth and the transitory nature of her attraction to the wrong man were somehow rooted in truth. She hadn't, back then, been sure enough of herself to resist the wisdom of the two people she trusted and loved.

Surely time would make her see sense and make her forget Javier and the new, wonderful feelings he had roused in her?

It wasn't as though she didn't *like* Roger, after all…

But it hadn't turned out that way. Neither of them had been able to find a way through all the muddy water under the bridge and she had discovered fast enough how easy it was for loathing to set in, forging a destructive path through affection and friendship.

She hadn't turned him on and he, certainly, had never, ever had the sort of effect on her that Javier was now having.

It was suddenly very, very important that they do this. Would he walk away if he knew that she was a virgin? Was he hoping for someone experienced, as he doubtless assumed she was, who could perform all sorts of exciting gymnastics in bed?

In her head, she balanced the scales.

Alarm and disappointment with her if he found out that he was dealing with someone who might not live up to expectation…versus her embarrassment at having to come clean and tell him the truth about the marriage into which she should never have entered…

Which in turn would lead her down all sorts of uncertain routes. Because how else could she explain away her mistake without letting him know just how much she had felt for him all those years ago, how deeply she had fallen in love with him?

And, in turn, would that lead him to start thinking that she might just go and do the same again, after he had issued his warnings and told her that this was just sex and nothing more—no romance, no courtship and certainly no repeat performance of what they had once had?

'I've never done this before.' She couldn't face the embarrassment of him pulling away, appalled that he had mistaken her for someone else, someone who might prove to be fun in bed instead of a novice waiting to be taught, guided only by instinct.

It took a few seconds for Javier to register what she had just said and he paid attention to her words only because of the tone in which they had been spoken.

He was still confused, though, as he pulled back to stare down at her.

'You mean you've never had a one-night stand with an ex-flame?'

'No.' Face flaming with embarrassment, she wriggled into a sitting position and drew the duvet cover protectively over her, suddenly shy in the face of his probing dark eyes.

'What, then?' He had never talked so much in bed

with any woman. Frustrated, he raked his fingers through his hair and sighed. 'Do I need to get dressed to sit this one out?'

'What are you talking about?'

'What I'm asking is…is this going to be a long conversation involving more confidence sharing? Should I make myself a pot of tea and settle down for the long haul?'

'Why do you have to be so sarcastic?' Sophie asked, stung.

'Because,' Javier pointed out coolly, 'this should be a simple situation, Sophie. Once upon a time, there was something between us. Now there isn't—aside, that is, from the small technicality that we never actually made it past the bedroom door. Indeed, we never made it even near the bedroom door. So here we are, rectifying that oversight before going our separate ways. I'm not sure that there's anything much to talk about because it's not one of those *getting to know you* exercises.'

'I know! You've already told me that. Not that you needed to! I don't have any illusions as to why we're here…and *I know* it's not because we're *getting to know one another*!' Which didn't mean that it didn't hurt to have it laid out so flatly. 'I don't *want to get to know you*, Javier!'

Javier frowned. 'What is that supposed to mean?'

'It means that you're not the sort of guy I could ever be interested in now.'

Did that bother him? No. Why should it? 'Explain!' And if he wanted an explanation, it was simply to indulge his curiosity. Perfectly understandable.

'You're arrogant.' She ticked off on one finger. 'You're condescending. You think that, because you have stacks of money, you can say whatever you want and do whatever you please. You can't even be bothered to make a show of being polite because you don't think you ever have to be...'

Javier was outraged. 'I can't believe I'm hearing this!' He leapt out of the bed to pace the floor, glaring at the shabby wallpaper and the crumbling cornices.

Sophie watched him, shocked at what she had just said but in no way having the slightest intention of taking any of it back. She had to keep her eyes glued to his face because that glorious body of his was still doing things to her, even in the middle of the sudden squall that had blown up between them.

'That's because I bet no one has the courage to ever criticise you.'

'That's ridiculous! I *invite* openness from my staff! In fact, I welcome positive criticism from everyone!'

'Maybe you forgot to tell them.' Sophie glared. 'Because you behave just like someone who has the rack on standby for anyone who dares speak their mind!'

'Maybe...' He strolled towards the bed and then leant over, caging her in, hands on either side of her. 'You're the only one who thinks there's room for improvement in me...'

'Arrogant! Do you honestly think you're *that perfect*?'

'I haven't had complaints,' he purred, suddenly turned on and invigorated by the heat between them. 'Especially from the opposite sex. Stop arguing, Soph. And stop talking...'

There was no way he was going to allow her to dance around this any longer.

And she didn't want to.

She met his eyes steadily and took a deep breath. 'You're not going to believe this…'

'I loathe when people open a sentence with that statement.'

'I've never slept with anyone before, Javier. I'm… I'm still a virgin…'

CHAPTER EIGHT

'DON'T BE RIDICULOUS.' He shot her a look of amused disbelief. 'You can't be.'

Sophie continued to stare at him until he frowned as he continued to grapple with her bolt-from-the-blue remark.

'And there's no need to try to pique my interest by pretending,' he crooned softly. 'My interest is already piqued. In fact, my interest was piqued the second your brother walked through the door with his begging bowl and sob story...'

'What are you saying? Are you telling me that... that...?'

'I suddenly realised what had been missing for the past seven years—completion.'

'You wanted us to end up in bed?'

'I knew we would.'

'Is that why you offered to help us?' Sophie edged away from him, shaking with anger. 'Because you wanted...*completion*?'

'Why are you finding that so hard to believe?' Javier couldn't believe that the tide had turned so swiftly.

One minute, he had been touching her, and now here she was, spinning him some tall story about being a virgin and staring at him as though he had suddenly transformed into the world's most wanted.

'I'm surprised…' she said bitterly, grabbing clothes from the floor and hopping into them, beyond caring that he was watching her dress and wishing that he would follow suit and do the same '…that you didn't try to blackmail me into bed by offering me a deal in return!' Silence greeted this remark and she paused and stared up at him through narrowed eyes that were spitting fire.

'You thought about it, though, didn't you…?' she said slowly.

'This is a ridiculous conversation.' Javier slipped on his boxers and moved to stand by the window, arms folded, his expression thunderous.

'Did you pick all that stuff for the flat? I wondered about that, wondered how come everything seemed to have a personal touch when you didn't actually live there. When your taste, judging from your office, didn't run to old-fashioned… Did you think that shoving me into free accommodation where I'd be surrounded by stuff that made me feel at home was a good way to butter me up into sleeping with you, so that you could have your *completion*?'

Javier flushed darkly and glowered. 'Since when is it a criminal offence to choose what to put in your own property?'

'I'm going to add *manipulative and underhand* to *arrogant and full of yourself*!' He was all those things *and more*, yet she still couldn't tear her eyes away from his masculine perfection as he remained standing with his back to the window, which just went to show how downright *unfair* fate could be.

She should throw him out of the house, tell him what he could do with his deal and order him never to darken her doors again.

Instead, the awful truth was sinking in…

She still wanted him, still wanted to sleep with him, and for her it wasn't all about completion, even though that was what she had told herself, because that was the acceptable explanation for what she felt.

For her…

A jumble of confused, mixed-up emotions poured through her, weakening her, and she feebly pushed them aside because she didn't want to dwell on them.

Javier walked slowly towards her, half-naked, bronzed, a thing of such intense beauty that it took her breath away.

'So I weighted the scales in my favour,' he murmured. 'Where's the crime in that?' He was standing right in front of her now and he could almost *feel* the war raging inside her. Flee or stay put?

She wasn't running.

Because, like it or not, she wanted him as much as he wanted her and getting all worked up about the whys and hows didn't make a scrap of difference. The power of lust.

'I'm accustomed to getting what I want and I want you. And, yes, I did consider holding the offer of financial help over your head in exchange for that glorious body that has disturbed far too many of my nights, but I didn't.'

'Arrogant…' Sophie muttered. But she reluctantly had to concede that at least he wasn't trying to economise with the truth and the fact that he had used whatever ploys he had at hand to get what he wanted was all just part and parcel of his personality. There wasn't a scrap of shame or sheepishness in his voice.

He shrugged and smiled. 'Tell me you don't like it.'

'No one likes arrogance.' Her heart was beating madly. In the space of a heartbeat, the atmosphere had shifted right back to the sexy intimacy they had been sharing only moments earlier, before everything had gone downhill.

Before she had told him that she was a virgin.

'I've always been arrogant and you weren't complaining seven years ago. Why did you tell me that you were a virgin?'

'Because it's the truth,' she whispered stiltedly. 'I know you probably find that hard to believe.'

'Try impossible.'

'Roger…he…'

She wasn't lying or making up something to try to pique his interest. She was telling the truth. He could see it in her face and hear it in the clumsy awkwardness of her voice.

'Sit down.'

'Sorry?'

'You look as though you're about to collapse.' He guided her away from the bed with all its heated connotations of sex towards a chair that was by the window, facing into the room. Perhaps she sat there in the light evenings and read a book. It was the sort of thing he could picture her doing.

What he *couldn't* picture her doing was marrying some man only to spend her married life in a state of frustrated virginity.

Who the hell did something like that?

'You hadn't slept with the man before you…agreed to walk up the aisle with him?' This when she was sitting on the chair like a fragile wooden doll and he had dragged over the only other chair in the room, which had been in front of the oversized, dark mahogany dressing table.

'He… I…' The weight of all those nagging thoughts that she had temporarily pushed aside surged forward in a rush that made her breath hitch in her throat. She couldn't even remember what she had expected from her doomed marriage to Roger. She had half believed her parents when they had told her that her feelings for Javier were just an adolescent crush, the result of being away from home, being free for the first time in her young life. It happened to everyone, they had insisted, and it would blow over in due course. She would gravitate back towards someone on her own level, from her own social class, and the thrill of the unknown would fade away in time.

They had been very convincing, and as all those other reasons for marrying Roger had piled up, so had the tug of war going on inside her intensified.

But had she ever foreseen a satisfying sex life with the man she should never have wed?

Had she properly considered what married life was going to be like for her? Had she simply assumed that forgetting Javier would be as easy as her parents had said it would be and so all those feelings would, likewise, be easily replaced, transferred to Roger? What a complete idiot she had been! Foolish and naïve.

She now knew that what she had felt for Javier hadn't been a passing crush. She had fallen in love with him and he had been spot on when he had told her, just then, that his arrogance had never bothered her when they had been going out.

It was just something else she had adored about him. That and his utter integrity, his dry wit, his sharp intelligence and his sense of fair play.

She was still in love with him and all those traits that should have turned her off him but didn't. He had become the billionaire he had quietly always known he would end up being, and of course he had changed in the process. How could he not? But underneath the changes was the same man and she was still in love with him.

And just acknowledging that appalled and frightened her.

Because things might have stayed the same for her but they hadn't stayed the same for him.

He really did want completion. He hadn't stayed celibate over the years. He was a powerful, wealthy man now who could have any woman on the planet with a snap of his fingers. She was the one who'd got away, and he was determined to put that right, so he was having a little time out with her.

He didn't love her and whatever feelings he had had for her in the past had disappeared over the years. He'd made that perfectly clear. But she still loved him and that was a dreadful state of affairs.

Whilst one part of her realised that she must look very strange, just sitting with a blank expression on her face, another part recognised that there was nothing she could do about that because she couldn't control the racing whirlpool of her thoughts.

One thing was emerging very fast, though. She couldn't let him know how she felt. If he could be cool and controlled, then she must be as well. There was no way that she would allow him to see just how weak and vulnerable she was inside.

'There's no need to explain,' Javier said gently. He was beginning to feel all sorts of things and top of the list was intense satisfaction that he was going to be her first. He'd never thought that he was the sort of primal guy who would actually be thrilled to the core by something like that but he had clearly underestimated his own primitive side. Under the civilised veneer, he was as untamed as they came.

'What…what do you mean?' Sophie stammered. Of course, he had no insight into her murky past, but she still had a moment of wondering whether he had somehow worked everything out, including her feelings for him.

'I don't suppose you ever anticipated entering into a sexless marriage.'

Sophie went beetroot-red and didn't snatch back her

hand when he reached out and idly played with her fingers.

'I...er...I...'

'No.' He stopped her mid awkward sentence. 'Like I said, there's no need to explain because I understand.'

'You do?'

'You were young. You weren't to know that it takes all sorts to make the world go round and some men find it harder than others to face their sexuality.'

'Sorry?'

For the first time in living memory, Javier wasn't seeing red when he thought about the loser she had tossed him over for. In many ways, he felt sorry for her. With financial problems surfacing on the home front, and a man with control over purse strings her family needed, she had failed to see that he had his own agenda and had tied the knot in the expectation that life would be normal.

She'd been sorely mistaken.

Javier shunted aside thorny questions about whether she had loved the guy or not. That was then and this was now and, in the interim, she sure as hell had had her wake-up call on that front.

A virgin widow and now here she was. Here they both were...

Sophie was reeling from the series of misunderstandings and misinterpretations. Red-blooded alpha male that Javier was, he had jumped to the simplest conclusion. She was good-looking, she and Roger had married... The only possible reason they might not have consummated their marriage would be because he physically hadn't been able to, and the only reason that might have been the case would be because he just wasn't attracted to women.

End of story.

Was she going to set him straight on that count? Was she going to tell him the series of events that had led to her sexless union? The depth of feeling she had carried for him, Javier? Was she going to risk him knowing how madly in love with him she had been and then finding the link and working out just how madly in love she still was with him?

'Roger, gay...' He might as well have been for the amount of notice he had paid her.

'Key thing here is this, Soph—it was nothing you did.'

'Really?' She very much doubted that but Javier nodded briskly.

'I went out with a functioning alcoholic a couple of years ago,' he confided, drawing her closer to him and liking her lack of resistance. 'You would never have guessed that she drank her daily intake of calories. She was a model with an erratic, hectic lifestyle and she was very careful.'

'Didn't you suspect anything?' Sophie stared at him, round-eyed. It was a relief to have the conversation off her for a moment.

'We were both busy, meeting in various foreign locations either where she was modelling or where I happened to be. I only twigged when she started having more ambitious plans for our...relationship.'

'What does that mean?'

'It means she decided that meeting in various foreign locations wasn't enough. She wanted something of a more permanent arrangement.'

'Poor woman,' Sophie said with heartfelt sympathy.

'Misplaced sympathies,' Javier said wryly. 'She knew the game before it started. Not my fault if somewhere along the line she forgot the rules.'

She knew the game the way I know the game, Sophie thought, *and I'd better make sure I don't forget the rules or else...*

And with a finger in the family company—frankly more than just a finger—parting company might be a little more difficult than he would want. Not just a simple case of ignoring calls and text messages after signing off with a bunch of flowers and a thanks-but-no-thanks farewell note...

'So how did you, er, find out that there was a problem?'

'She surprised me by inviting me over to her place in London for dinner.'

'And it was the first time you'd been there?'

'Like I said, the rules of the game…they don't include cosy domestic scenes.'

'You eat out all the time?'

Javier shrugged. 'It works. I'm only interested in the bedroom when it comes to any woman's house.'

Sophie thought that he'd seen more than just the bedroom of this particular house, but then, she knew, circumstances weren't exactly typical even though the ground rules would be exactly the same.

'But I went along and it didn't take me long to see just how many bottles of alcohol there were in places where food should have been stored. And it took even less time to unearth the mother lode because there had been no reason for her to hide any of it as she didn't share the flat with anyone. When I confronted her, she tried to make me believe that it was somehow my fault that she drank as much as she did, because I wouldn't commit to her. She clung and cried and said that her drinking had gone through the roof because she was depressed that our relationship wasn't going anywhere. Of course, I left her immediately and then got in touch with a private counsellor specialising in people with alcohol-related addictions. But the point I'm making is that there are just some people who won't face up to their own shortcomings and will take every opportunity to shift the blame onto other people.'

'And you think that, er, that Roger…'

'I think nothing.' Javier gestured in a way that was exotically foreign and then leant in closer to her. 'It would be a tough call for a man to find the courage to face up to his own sexual inclinations when those sexual inclinations risk putting him outside his comfort zone and alienating him from the people he has grown up with.'

'Roger was certainly a coward,' Sophie said bitterly.

'But all that is in the past.' He waved his hand elegantly. 'We find ourselves here and I'm glad you felt comfortable enough to bare all to me.'

'You would have found out anyway,' she said vaguely.

'You shouldn't have put your clothes back on. Now I'm going to have to strip them off you all over again.

No, scrap that—what I'd really like is for you to take them off for me, bit by slow bit, a piece at a time, so that I can appreciate every delectable bit of your glorious body…'

'I…I can't do that.'

'You're shy…' Had she ever undressed in front of her husband? he wondered. Was all of this completely new to her? He confessed to himself that he was tickled pink and turned on like hell by the thought of that, the thought of him being the absolute first on so many counts.

Shy but unbelievably turned on…

She liked the way his dark, appreciative eyes roved over her like a physical caress. She liked the way he made her feel. She had never done any kind of striptease for a man before but now she began undressing as he had asked, very slowly, eyes never leaving his as she removed her clothing.

He made her feel safe and she knew why. It was because she loved him. She knew that he could hurt her beyond repair—knew that her love would never be returned and, after tonight, she would be left with only the memory of making love and the knowledge that what she wanted would never happen—but none of that seemed to matter. She'd thought that her heart could never again be made to beat but she'd been wrong. Her love overrode common sense and she couldn't fight it.

And what was the point of fighting anyway? She lived with enough regret on her shoulders without adding to the tally. If she had this one opportunity to grasp a bit of happiness, then why shouldn't she take it? She would deal with the aftermath later.

She unhooked her bra, stepped out of her undies and then walked slowly towards him, sashaying provocatively and seeing for herself the effect she was having on him.

Javier held his erection through his boxers, controlling the wayward effects of his surging libido. He breathed deeply and tried to think pleasant, pedestrian thoughts so that he could gather himself sufficiently to do justice to the situation.

No rushing.

'You look tense,' Sophie murmured. She was amazed at how at ease she was with her nakedness. Indeed, she was positively basking in it. She delicately stroked the side of his face with one finger and Javier grabbed it and sucked it, watching her with smouldering passion so that every bone in her body seemed to go into meltdown.

'*Tense* isn't quite the word I would use...' He drew her close to him so that their bodies were lightly pressed together and, eyes still locked to hers, he eased his hand over her hip, along her thigh and then between them.

Her wetness on his finger elicited a moan of pure satisfaction from him.

Sophie couldn't breathe. Her eyelids fluttered. There was something so erotic about them both standing, looking at one another while he rubbed his finger against the small, tight bud of her clitoris, rousing sensations like little explosions and fireworks inside her. She shifted and moaned softly.

'This is just the appetiser,' Javier murmured, kissing her on her mouth, small, darting kisses that left her breathless. 'And there will be lots of those to enjoy before the main course.'

'I want to pleasure you too…'

'You already are. Trust me—just touching you is giving me more pleasure than you could even begin to understand.'

In one fluid movement, he swept her off her feet and carried her to the bed as easily as if she weighed nothing. He deposited her as gently as if she were a piece of priceless porcelain and then he stood back and looked at her, and Sophie looked back at him, eyes half-closed, her breathing shallow and jerky. The outline of his impressive erection made her heart skip a beat.

She realised that she had never actually considered the dynamics of sexual intercourse; how something so big would fit into her…

'Your face is as transparent as a sheet of glass,' Javier told her drily. 'There's no need to be nervous. I am going to be very gentle.'

'I know you will.' And she did. He might be ruthless on the battlefield of high finance, but here in the bedroom he was a giver and utterly unselfish. That was something she sensed.

Javier decided that he would leave the boxers on. He didn't want to scare her. He was a big boy and he had seen that flash of apprehension on her face and interpreted it without any difficulty at all. He'd said he was going to be gentle and he would be; he would ease himself into her and she would accept his largeness without anything but sheer, unadulterated pleasure.

He had forgotten that this single act was supposed to be about revenge.

He positioned her arms above her head and she shifted into the position so that her breasts were pointing at him. Hunkering over her, he delicately circled one rosy nipple with his tongue until she was writhing in response.

'No moving,' he chastised sternly. 'Or else I might have to tie those hands of yours together above your head…'

'You wouldn't.' But now that he had put that thought in her head, she found that she rather enjoyed playing around with it in her mind.

Maybe another time, she thought with heated contentment only to realise that there wouldn't *be* another time. This was it. This was all he wanted. A night of fun so that he could get the *completion* he felt he deserved.

She felt a sharp, searing pain as she pictured him walking away from her, taking his sense of completion with him, returning to the queue of beautiful, experienced women patiently waiting for him.

She squeezed her eyes tightly shut, blocking out the intrusive, unwelcome image and succumbing to the riot of physical sensations sparked as he trailed kisses along her collarbone, down to her pouting, pink nipple.

He took his time. He drew her aching nipple into his mouth so that he could caress the tip with his tongue in firm, circular movements that had her gasping for breath. Every time she lowered her arm to clutch his hair, he pushed it back up without pausing in his devastating caress.

'Now let's try this another way,' he murmured, rising up and staring down at her flushed, drowsy face.

'I'm not pleasing you...' Sophie's voice was suddenly anxious and her eyes expressed concern that she was taking without giving anything in return.

'Shh...' Javier admonished. 'Like I said, you're doing more for me than you can ever imagine possible.' *Doing more than any woman had ever done before.*

She made him feel young again. He was no longer the boy who had grown into a man whose only focus was forging the financial stability he had grown up wanting. He was no longer the tycoon who had made it to the top, who could have anything and anyone he wanted. He was young again, without the cynicism invested in him by his upwards journey.

'Straddle me,' he commanded, flipping her so that their positions were reversed, and she was now the one over him, her full breasts dangling like ripe fruit, swinging tantalisingly close to his face. 'And move on me...move on my thigh...let me feel your wetness...'

Sophie obeyed. It was wickedly decadent. She moved against his thigh, slowly and firmly, legs parted so that she could feel the nudge of an orgasm slowly building.

She didn't care that he could see the naked, openmouthed lust on her face or hear the heavy, laboured breathing which she could no longer get under control.

She didn't care if he watched her, in her most private moment, come against his leg.

She was so turned on, she could scarcely breathe.

She gasped when he held her breasts, massaging their fullness, drawing her down towards him so that he could suckle on first one, then the other, while she continued to pleasure herself against him, hands pinned on either side of him.

As limp as a rag doll, she lay for a while on him, taking time out to quell the rise of an impending orgasm because she wanted to have it all. She didn't want to come like this. She wanted to feel him moving hard in her.

The apprehension she had earlier felt when she had seen his impressive size had faded completely.

He was in no rush. He stroked her spine and then, when she propped herself up once again, he kissed her slowly, tasting every morsel of her mouth. Her hair fell around her and he pushed his hand through its tangle and gazed at her in perfect, still silence.

'You're beautiful, Sophie.'

Sophie blushed, unused to compliments. She felt as though she had given away her carefree youth somewhere along the line and that single compliment had returned it to her for a little while.

'I bet you say that to all the women you get into bed with.' Her voice was soft and breathless and he quirked an eyebrow in amusement.

'Is that the sound of someone fishing for compliments?'

Sophie thought that actually it was the sound of someone trying to be casual when in fact she was eaten up with jealousy over lovers she had never met or seen.

'It's been a very long time since anyone paid me a

compliment,' she told him truthfully and for a few moments Javier stared at her seriously.

'Weren't you tempted to get some sort of life of your own after your husband died? Or even when he was alive, given the extraordinary circumstances?'

Sophie felt a distinct twinge of guilt that she had allowed him to believe something that couldn't have been further from the truth. But then she reminded herself that she was simply avoiding opening a can of worms and where was the harm in a very small white lie? It hardly altered the fact that she was a virgin, did it?

She decided to completely skirt around the whole thorny business of life as she had known it when she had been married to Roger.

'By the time my husband died,' she said instead, snuggling against him, 'I was so snowed under with financial problems, I barely had time to eat a meal and brush my teeth, never mind launch myself into the singles scene and start trying to find a man.'

'And you must have been pretty jaded with the male sex by then,' Javier offered encouragingly.

'Um…with life in general,' she returned vaguely.

'And with your husband specifically,' Javier pressed. 'Understand one hundred percent—he lied and used you and on top of that managed to ruin what was left of your family company.'

Sophie sighed. Put like that, she marvelled that she had had the strength to go on after her mother had moved down to Cornwall. She marvelled that she just hadn't thrown in the towel and fled to the furthest corners of the earth to live on a beach somewhere.

She had been raised to be dutiful and responsible, however, and she could see now, looking back on her life, that those two traits, whilst positive, had in fact been the very things that had taken her down the wrong road. At the age of just nineteen, she had been dutiful and responsible enough to put herself last so that she could fall in line with what everyone else seemed to want from her.

'Let's not talk about all that,' she said gruffly, sensing the tears of self-pity not too far away. What a fantastic start to her one big night that would be—snotty nosed, puffy eyed and blubbing like a baby in front of him!

It enraged Javier that she still couldn't seem to find it in herself to give the man the lack of due credit and respect he so richly deserved, even with a string of unpalatable facts laid out in front of her. But, he thought with harsh satisfaction, who was she here with now? Him! And he was going to take her to such heights that by the time he walked away from her he would be the only man in her head. No one forgot their first lover.

'You're right,' he breathed huskily, expertly reversing positions so that he was the dominant one now, on top of her. 'I've always found talking superfluous between the sheets...'

Sophie sadly thanked her lucky stars that she had ended her rambling conversation before she could really begin to bore him witless. If he didn't care for women talking when they were in bed with him, then she shuddered to think what he might feel if she began weeping like a baby and clutching him like a life jacket flung into stormy seas to a drowning man.

Javier lowered himself and began to kiss her. He started with her mouth and he took his time there, until she was whimpering and squirming, then he moved to her succulent breasts, nibbling and nipping and suckling. Her skin was like satin, velvety smooth and warm. When he began to lick her stomach, her sides, the path down to her belly button, she moaned with fevered impatience.

She reached down compulsively and tangled her fingers in his hair.

'Javier!'

Sophie met his darkened gaze and blushed furiously. 'What…are you doing?'

'Trust me,' he murmured roughly. 'I'm taking you to heaven…' He gently pushed her thighs open and she fell back, then sucked in a shocked breath. The delicate darting of his tongue as he explored her was agonisingly, explosively erotic.

She moved against his mouth, rocking and undulating her hips, and groaning so loudly that it was a blessing the house was empty. She arched up, pushing herself into that slickly exploring tongue, and cried out when two fingers, gently inserted into her wetness, ratcheted up the wildly soaring sensations racing through her as fast as quicksilver.

'I'm going to…' She could scarcely get the words out before a shattering orgasm ripped through her and she clutched the sheets, driving herself upwards as his big hands supported her tightened buttocks.

It was an orgasm that went on and on, taking her to heights she had never dreamed possible, before subsiding, returning her gently back to planet Earth.

She scrambled onto her elbows, intent on apologising for being so selfish, but Javier was already out of the bed and rooting through his trousers.

It was only when he began putting on protection that it dawned on her what he was doing.

The last thing he would want was a pregnancy.

She barely had time to register the treacherous stab of curiosity that filled her head... *What would a baby created by them look like?*

'Lie back,' he urged with a wolfish grin. 'The fun is only beginning...'

CHAPTER NINE

SOPHIE QUIVERED WITH anticipation but this time it was her decision to take things slowly. He had pleasured her in the most intimate and wonderful way possible and now it was her turn to give.

She wriggled so that she was kneeling and gently pushed him so that he was lying down. His initial expression of surprise quickly gave way to one of wicked understanding that she wanted the opportunity to take the reins instead of leaving it all to him.

'No touching,' she whispered huskily.

'That's going to be impossible.'

'You're going to have to fold your hands behind your head.' She grinned and then looked at him with haughty reprimand. 'It's only what *you* asked *me* to do.'

'Well, then,' he drawled, 'I'd better obey, hadn't I?' He lay back, arms folded behind his head. He could have watched that glorious body for ever, the shapely indent of her waist, the full heaviness of her breasts, the perfect outline of her nipples, the scattering of freckles along her collarbone, that tiny mole on the side of her left breast…

Her eyes were modestly diverted but he knew that she was aware of him with every ounce of her being and that was a real turn on for him.

He'd never felt so *alive* to the business of making love. Somehow, he was functioning on another level, where every sensation was heightened to almost unbearable limits.

Was it because he was finally making love to the one woman who had escaped him? Was this what it felt like finally to settle old scores?

Would he be feeling this had he had her the first time round? No. That was a given. However crazy he'd been about her, he knew far more about himself now than he had back then. He knew that he wasn't cut out for permanence. If they had slept together, carried on seeing one another, if circumstances hadn't interrupted their relationship, it still wouldn't have lasted. Because, whether he liked it or not, he'd been focused on one thing and one thing only—the acquisition of the sort of wealth that would empower him, afford him the financial security he had never had growing up.

He no longer questioned his motivation, if indeed he ever had. Some things were ingrained, like scores from a branding iron, and that was one of them.

He had no burning desire for children and not once, over the years, had any of the women he had dated given him pause for thought. He expected that if he ever married—and it was a big *if*—it would be a marriage of convenience, a union years down the road with a suitable woman who would make him an acceptable companion with whom to see in his retirement. A woman of independent means, because the world was full of gold-diggers, who enjoyed the same things he enjoyed and would make no demands on him. He would look for a harmonious relationship.

Harmony in his fading years would be acceptable. Until then, he would make do with his string of women, all beautiful, all amenable, all willing to please and all so easily placated with jewellery and gifts if he ended up being unreliable.

They were all a known quantity and, in a life driven by ambition, it was soothing to have a private life where there were no surprises.

Except, right now, Sophie was the exception to the rule, and a necessary exception.

And he was enjoying every minute of her.

She straddled him and he looked down, to the slickness between her legs, and then up as she leant over him so that she could tease his hungry mouth with her dangling breasts.

He was allowed to lick, but only for a while, and allowed to suckle, but only for a while.

And he wasn't allowed to touch, which meant he had to fight off the agonising urge to pull her down so that she was on top of him and take her.

She did to him what he had done to her. She explored his torso with her mouth. She kissed the bunched muscles of his shoulders and then circled his flat, brown nipples with her mouth so that she could drizzle her tongue over them with licks as dainty as a cat's.

She could feel the demanding throb of his erection against her but it was only when she moved lower down his body that she circled its massive girth with her hand, pressing down firmly and somehow knowing what to do, how to elicit those groans from him, how to sharpen his breathing until each breath was accompanied by a shudder.

Instinct.

Or something else. Love. Love that had been born all those years ago and had forgotten that it was supposed to die. Like a weed, it had clung and survived the worst possible conditions so that now it could resume its steady growth. Against all odds and against all better judgement.

Well, worse conditions loomed round the corner, but before she encountered those she would enjoy this night to the absolute fullest.

She straightened, eyes dark with desire, and half-smiled with a sense of heady power as she registered his utter lack of control. She might be the inexperienced one here, but when it came to the power of *lust* she wasn't the only one to be in its grip. She wasn't the only one who was out of control.

And that balanced the scales a bit.

Hot and consumed with a sense of recklessness she would never have thought possible, she sat astride him so that he could breathe in the musky scent of her, positioning herself over him so that he could explore between her legs with his flicking tongue.

She breathed in sharply as he found her sensitive clitoris and probed it with the tip of his tongue.

He still wasn't touching her, still had his hands behind his head, as she had her fists clenched at her sides.

But the heat between them was indescribable all the more so because of the tantalising promise of fulfilment that lay ahead.

She let him taste her until she could stand it no longer, until her breathing was so fractured that she wanted to scream. She could move against his mouth but there was no way she was going to come again, not like this…

She worked her way down him until she was the one tasting him. The solid steel of his erection fascinated her. She took it into her mouth, sucked on the tip, played with it with her hands, tasted it and loved the way it tasted.

She explored his hard six-pack with the flat of her hand as she sucked, enjoying the hard, abrasive rub of muscle and sinew under her palm.

'Okay.' Javier rose onto his elbows to tangle his hand in her tumbling hair. 'Enough. My blood pressure can't take any more.'

Sophie glanced at him from under her lashes.

'You're a witch,' he breathed huskily. 'Come here and kiss me.'

Their kiss was a mingling of scents and Sophie lost herself in it. She wanted to wrap her arms around him and never let him go. She wanted to be needy, clingy and demanding, and all those awful things that would have him running for the hills without a backwards glance.

She wanted to be open and honest, tell him how she felt and declare her love for him, and the fact that there was no way that she could do that felt like an impossible weight on her shoulders.

She sighed, rolling as he propelled her gently onto her back. Balancing over her, he looked at her seriously.

'Still nervous?'

'A little,' she admitted. She could have admitted a lot more. She could have admitted that what really made her nervous was the prospect of what happened when this glorious night was over and they both returned to their own little worlds. There was no way she would duck away from this but the aftermath still made her nervous.

She didn't think he would like to hear about that.

'Don't be,' he murmured. 'Trust me.'

He nudged her with the tip of his erection, felt her wetness and gently, slowly eased himself in.

She was beautifully tight. Would he have guessed that she had never made love before? Probably. She would have winced, given her inexperience away. That said, he was pleased that she had thought to confide in him and more than pleased that he was going to be her first lover.

Whatever feelings still lingered for the creep who had married her for all the wrong reasons, *he* would be the man who would be imprinted in her head for the rest of her life. Not her ex-husband. When she lay in bed, the loser she still refused to hold in contempt would no longer dominate her thoughts. No. Instead, *he* would be in her head now, and the memory of this first night spent together.

Sophie inhaled and tensed but she was already so turned on that the tension quickly evaporated. Nor did she want him treating her like a piece of china that could shatter into a thousand pieces if he happened to be just a little too rough.

She wanted him to thrust long and deep into her. She wanted his *urgency*.

'Move faster...' she moaned.

It was all the invitation Javier needed. He was unbelievably aroused. Holding on had required a superhuman feat of willpower because having her touch him had driven him wild.

He began moving with expert assurance, felt her wince as he drove deeper, then gradually relax as he picked up pace until their bodies were moving in harmony, as sweet as the coming together of the chords of a song.

Still, he refused to satisfy himself at her expense, waiting until her rhythm was inexorably building and he could feel her fingers dig into the small of his back and knew that she had raised her legs, wrapped them around his waist, all the better to receive him...

Sophie came, spinning off to a different world where nothing existed but her body and its powerful, shattering responses. She was distantly aware of Javier arching up, his whole body tensing as he reached orgasm.

Apart yet inextricably joined. She had never felt closer to anyone in her entire life. And it wasn't just because of the sex. Somewhere in the core of her she knew that it was what it was because of what she felt. She couldn't disentangle her emotions from her responses. The two were inextricably linked.

Not good. Yet so right. She couldn't imagine feeling anything like this for anyone else, ever, and that scared her because when this was over she would have no choice but to pick up the pieces and move on. She would have to put him behind her and one day find herself a partner because she couldn't envisage spending the rest of her life on her own.

She was lying in the crook of his arm, both of them staring upwards. His breathing was thick and uneven and with a little chuckle he swung her onto her side so that they were now facing one another, their bodies pressed together.

Somewhere along the line he had disposed of the condom. He was a very generously built man, however, and even with his erection temporarily subsided she was still aware of his thick length against her, stirring her, although she was aching a little and as tired as if she had run a marathon at full tilt.

She wondered what the protocol was for a one-night stand. She couldn't leap out of bed, stroll to get her clothes and head for the door, having thanked him for a good time, because it was her house. Which meant that she would have to rely on him to make the first move, and that made her feel a little awkward, because she didn't want him to imagine that she was hanging around, waiting for an encore.

She was afraid to carry on being intimate, in these most intimate of circumstances, because she didn't want him to guess the depth of her feelings for him.

She wanted to maintain her dignity. It wasn't just a case of self-preservation, but on a more realistic level: he now had a slice of the family company. He might decide to take a back seat now that they had made love and *completion* had been established, might disappear never to be seen again, but on the small chance that she bumped into him at some point in the future the last thing she needed was for him to know her feelings. If she bumped into him, she wanted him to think that she had been as detached from the whole experience, on an emotional level, as he had been. She wanted to be able to have a conversation with him, with her head held high, and preferably with a man on her arm.

'So,' Javier drawled, breaking the silence and stroking her hair away from her face.

'So...' Sophie cleared her throat and offered him a bright smile. 'That was very nice.'

Javier burst out laughing. 'That's a first,' he informed her wryly. 'I've never had a woman tell me afterwards that the sex was "very nice".'

Sophie didn't want to think about the women he had bedded or what sexy little conversations they had had post–making love.

'You don't have to tell me that.' She was going to keep it light, brace herself for when he levered himself out of bed and began getting dressed. She didn't think he'd be spending the night.

'No?'

'I already have a picture in my head of the sort of women you, er, entertain and I guess they'd be busy telling you how great you were and offering to do whatever you wanted...'

'Did you think I was great?'

Sophie blushed a vibrant red.

'Is that a *yes*…?' He nuzzled her neck and then absently rested his hand between her legs.

'What happens about the shoot?'

'I don't want to talk about the shoot. I want to talk about how great you found me between the sheets.'

Sophie didn't want to laugh but her lips twitched because there was just something so incredibly endearing and boyish about his arrogance.

'I'm glad we made love,' she told him truthfully. 'I…'

'Don't go there, Soph.' He fell onto his back and gazed upwards because this was what he didn't want. Any sort of half-hearted, limp excuses and explanations for the choices she had made seven years ago. She'd already told him enough. He knew enough. He wasn't interested in hearing any more.

'Don't go where?'

'This isn't the point where we pick up sharing our life histories.' He gathered her into him, his arm draped loosely around her. He could touch her nipple with his fingers and he liked that. He liked the way the little bud stiffened in response to the gentle pressure of his fingers rolling it. And he liked what that did to his body, the way it made him feel as though he could keep going indefinitely, his body resting between bouts of lovemaking only long enough to build back up the vigour to carry on.

After sex, no matter how good the sex had been, his instinct had always been to get out of bed as fast as he could and have a shower, his mind already racing ahead to work and business, deals that had to be done.

He'd never been one for hanging around between the sheets, chewing the fat and talking about a future that wasn't going to happen.

But he wanted to hang around between the sheets now.

Minus the chat.

He'd managed, just, to relegate her loser ex-husband to a box somewhere in his head that he could safely ignore. The last thing he wanted was for her to begin recapping her past, forcing him to confront the unpalatable truth that, whether she had come to him a virgin or not, she had still ditched him for someone else and probably still loved that someone else, even though the man in question had failed to deliver.

'No,' she agreed quickly. 'I was simply going to say that it's probably a good idea if you head back now. Unfortunately…' she gave a derisive laugh '…the guest bedrooms aren't exactly made up for visiting crowds. No crisp white sheets and fluffy towels, I'm afraid.'

She began to slip her legs over the side of the bed and he tugged her back against him.

He wasn't ready for her to leave just yet. He hadn't quite got his fill of her. Surprising, all things considered, but nevertheless true. And he didn't want to give her time to think things over. He wanted her warm, ripe and soft like she was now; yielding.

'I'm not sure I can face the horror story of a long drive back to London,' he murmured, curving his big body against hers and pushing his thigh between her legs.

'There are hotels,' Sophie told him as her heart gave a silly little leap in her chest.

She didn't want him to go. It was exhausting pretending that she didn't care one way or another.

'This may be the back of beyond for you,' she carried on, 'compared to London, but we still have our fair share of excellent hotels. All come complete with mod cons like clean sheets, windows that open and no lingering smell of mustiness from being shut up for too long.'

Javier burst out laughing. He'd forgotten how funny she could be and that was something that hadn't been apparent over the past few weeks.

Probably over the past few years, he thought, sobering up.

'Bit of a trek going to a hotel,' he murmured. 'That would entail me getting up, getting dressed…and who's to say that they aren't all full?'

'What are you saying?'

'I could always save myself the hassle and spend the night here,' he told her.

'Some of the bedrooms… Well, I guess I could make up the one at the end of the corridor. It's shocking to think how fast things have gone downhill here…' She sighed. 'It's as if the whole place was glued together with sticking plaster and then, one day, someone tugged some of the plaster off and everything else just came down with it. Like a house of cards being toppled. I can't imagine the stress my dad had been living under for ages. It's as well he's not alive to see the way the house has gone downhill. And it's a blessing that Mum is down in Cornwall. She honestly doesn't know the half of what's been going on here.' She pulled back and looked at him gravely. 'Sorry. I forgot you don't like conversing between the sheets.'

'That's not what I said,' Javier felt constrained to mutter. But she had hit the nail on the head. It was all tied in with his driving need to focus on the essentials—work and financial security. For the first time, he found himself projecting to places beyond those confines, the sort of places most people seemed ridiculously keen to occupy, places which he had shunned as irrelevant. 'How can your mother not know what's been happening here?' he found himself asking. 'How often do you go down to Cornwall to visit her? She surely must return here on occasion?'

'Are you really interested? Because you don't have to ask a load of questions just because you happen to be staying on here for a few more hours.'

'So you're going to put me up?'

Sophie shrugged. 'It's no bother for me.'

'Good, because I'd quite like to have a look around the house in the morning—see how bad it is in the unforgiving light of day.'

'Why?' She propped herself up on one elbow and stared down at him.

'Curiosity. You were explaining the mystery of how it is that your mother doesn't know the situation here.'

'Would you like something to eat? To drink?'

'I'm fine here.'

But, even to her, chatting like this in bed felt weirdly intimate and she could understand why he avoided doing it. It would be easy to find herself being seduced into all sorts of cosy, inappropriate feelings, into thinking this was more than it actually was.

'Well, I'm starved,' she declared briskly, disentangling herself from him and scrambling for the door so that she could head to the bathroom for a shower.

Caught on the back foot, Javier frowned as he watched her hastily departing figure.

Since when did women turn down invitations from him to stay in bed—*talking*?

Actually, since when had he made a habit of issuing invitations to women to stay in bed, talking?

He levered himself out and strolled to the bathroom which was a couple of doors along. He was surprised that the bedrooms weren't all en suite and then surmised that the house predated such luxuries and, somewhere along the line, it had become too costly to have them installed.

He pushed open the door to the succulent sight of her bending over the bath to test the water.

Her hair was swept over one shoulder, the tips almost touching the water in the bath. She had one hand on the mixer tap, the other gripping the side of the cast-iron claw-foot bath. He could see the low hang of one breast swinging as she adjusted the temperature of the water, and he moved to stand behind her, grinning as she gave a little squeak when he straddled her from behind, cupping both breasts with his hands.

'Couldn't resist,' he murmured into her hair as she straightened and leant into him so that her back was pressed against his torso.

He massaged her breasts and bent to nibble and kiss

the slender column of her neck. With a sigh of contentment, Sophie closed her eyes and covered his hands
with hers.

'What are you doing?' she asked thickly.

'Is there any doubt?'

'I was just going to have a bath…then maybe get
something for us to eat.'

'I have all I want to eat right here, right now…'

Sophie moaned softly at the provocative image that
hoarsely spoken statement planted in her head.

They hadn't talked at all. Not really. Not about the
one thing they needed to talk about. Which was *what
happened next*. She knew that she shouldn't be sinking into his arms like this, should be maintaining some
distance, but her body was turning to liquid as he continued to assault her senses.

She could have locked the door, of course, but somehow that would have felt silly and childish after they
had just finished making love.

And maybe, she thought weakly, there was a part of
her that wouldn't have wanted to stop him from coming into the bathroom anyway.

She breathed in sharply as his wicked hand drifted
lower. Now he was just caressing one breast, playing with the pulsing, pink nipple while his other hand
roamed over her ribcage, exploring downwards at a
leisurely pace.

'Spread your legs,' he instructed softly and Sophie
obeyed, as weak as a kitten.

She knew what he was going to do, yet she still

gasped as he immediately found the swollen bud of her clitoris with the flat of his finger.

He knew just how to rub her there, applying just the right amount of pressure. His fingers were devastating. She could feel her wetness on his hand, and she reached behind her to hold his erection, although the angle was awkward and she couldn't begin to do half as much as she would have liked to.

And she didn't have time.

Because the rhythm of his touching grew faster, his fingers sending a million darting sensations flowing through her body until she was rocking under the impact of an orgasm, bucking against his hand, unable to contain her low groaning cries as she reached the point of utter physical fulfilment.

She spun round, blindly kissed his neck, just as he had done to her only minutes previously, and then she knelt in front of him, tossing her hair behind her, and took his rock-hard bigness into her mouth.

He tasted…like heaven.

She sucked him and he curled his fingers into her hair. She could feel his loss of self-control as she continued, sucking and licking him at the same time, her slender fingers gripping his erection, moving and massaging, working her own rhythm.

Javier had never felt so wildly out of control before. She was exciting him in ways no other woman ever had and he could no more control his own orgasm than he could have stopped the sun from rising or setting.

Spent, he pulled her back to her feet and for a few

seconds their bodies were entwined into beautiful, sated pleasure, the aftermath of their physical satisfaction.

'I might have to share that oversized bath with you,' he murmured, tilting her face so that he could gently kiss her on her mouth.

Sophie smiled, as content as a cat in possession of a full tub of cream.

This was just the sort of thing he might take for granted, think nothing of, but she was so scared of taking yet another step into *him*…into losing herself in a non-relationship that wasn't going anywhere and never would.

But what was the harm in having a bath with him? What was the harm in another first experience?

'Okay.'

'And then you can cook something for me to eat.' He had never uttered those words to any woman before.

'Don't expect cordon bleu food,' Sophie warned him in alarm and he laughed.

'Beans on toast would be fine.'

Sophie lowered herself into the water a little self-consciously, drawing her knees up as he took the other end. It was an enormous bath, easily accommodating the both of them, and he made a few approving noises as he settled into the water, pulling her legs out to tangle with his, looking for the inevitable signs of deterioration in the fabric of the building as he was now accustomed to doing after only a short space of time.

'Really?' she couldn't help but ask drily. Once upon a time, perhaps, but he was no longer a 'beans on toast' kind of guy.

'And then you can tell me about your mother and how you've managed to keep this situation from her.'

He stroked her calf, which sent a frisson rippling through her body. She literally couldn't seem to get enough of him and she marvelled at her body's capacity to rouse itself at the speed of light, from satiated, pleasant torpor to wakening hunger to be touched again.

'And then we can talk about this house, which appears to be on the point of collapse. But before all that you can wriggle up and turn round so that I can begin soaping you...'

Sophie looked at the newspaper spread out on the kitchen table in front of her.

It had been *that* easy to become accustomed to having him around. It had felt so natural. Working in London, having him in and out of the office, going through paperwork with him, sitting in on interviews, being consulted on absolutely everything to do with the company...

And then, when they were on their own, those precious times when they would talk, laugh, make love...

The company had picked up in the space of just a few short months. Swept along on the coat-tails of Javier and his remarkable reputation, business that had been lost to competitors was gradually returning and returning customers were treated to reward schemes that secured their loyalty.

Little changes had been incremental and she marvelled at how simple some of the solutions were to turn the company around.

With profit came money to start working on the house. And the profits had also secured Oliver's release from the work he had never enjoyed doing.

He had returned to America to become a sports teacher at one of the prestigious private schools.

Everything had slotted into place and, of course, she had grown complacent.

Who wouldn't have?

She had actually begun secretly to see a future for them, even though he never, ever made plans; never, ever mentioned doing anything with her at some point in the future.

The one-night stand had grown into a relationship that was now almost four months old.

They hadn't talked about Christmas but she could envisage them spending at least a part of it together.

All told, hope, that dangerous emotion, had begun to take root. Loving him had taken away her objectivity, made her vulnerable to all kinds of foolish thoughts about them having a proper relationship, a relationship in which he might actually be persuaded to try to make a go of it, persuaded to think about commitment.

It was her own fault for not listening to the dictates of common sense…

No sooner had she told herself that she had to maintain some sort of emotional distance than she had hurled herself headlong into a relationship that was the equivalent of a minefield.

And this was where it had got her.

She was driven to stare at the picture occupying a large portion of the tabloid newspaper she had bought on the spur of the moment from the local newsagent. Lord knew, she wasn't much of a newspaper reader. She had an app on her mobile that kept her fully updated with what was happening in the world.

The picture had been taken at a London gallery opening. She hadn't even known that Javier had been invited. Ensconced in Yorkshire, where she had been for the past couple of weeks, getting the local offices in order and supervising decorating and refurbishment, she had seen him in fits and starts.

She looked forward to his arrivals with eager, edge-of-seat anticipation. She dressed in clothes she imagined him ripping off. She no longer felt constrained to hide how much he turned her on. Lust and the physical side of things were the only things that were out in the open between them.

She knew how much he wanted her and he knew how much she wanted him.

And he was going to be arriving any minute now. She had cooked and could smell it wafting aromatically from the kitchen, which had seen recent updates and now functioned the way it once had, with everything working and in spanking new condition.

She neatly folded the paper and then hovered until, at seven promptly, she heard the insistent buzz of the doorbell. She closed her eyes and breathed in deeply to calm her shaky nerves.

She found that she'd even memorised the way he rang the doorbell, as if he couldn't wait to stride into the house, shedding his coat even as he reached to scoop her towards him.

She still hadn't become accustomed to that first sight of him. Even if she'd seen him the evening before, even if she'd seen him five minutes before, he still always blew her mind and took her breath away.

As always when he drove up north—quitting work earlier than he normally would because, he had confessed, those few hours behind the wheel of his car afforded him a certain amount of freedom which he deeply valued—he arrived still in his suit.

Minus jacket, which, she knew, he would have flung into the back seat of the car, oblivious to the fact that what he treated with such casual indifference had cost more than most people earned in a month.

'Have I told you that I missed you…?' Javier growled, closing the space between them in one fluid stride.

He had. It had been three days and he'd gone to sleep every evening with an erection and woken up with one. Not even those sexy phone calls late at night to her had been able to do the trick. There was only so much pleasure to be had satisfying himself.

He kissed her thoroughly, so thoroughly that Sophie forgot that this wasn't going to be the sort of evening they had both been anticipating: an evening of chat, food and lots of very satisfying sex. No, things were going to be different this evening because of that picture.

She pushed ever so slightly against him but immediately weakened as he plundered her mouth, driving her back until she was pressed against the wall.

She'd stopped wearing a bra in the house, liking the

fact that he could touch her whenever he wanted without the bother of removing it, and she hadn't thought to put one on this evening. Her head fell back as he pushed up her long-sleeved tee shirt to feel her.

He'd thought of nothing but her on the drive up and now to touch her breast, feel the tautness of her nipple between his fingers, was almost indescribable.

'I want to take you right here,' he confessed unsteadily. 'I don't even think I can make it to the bedroom. Or *any* room…'

'Don't be silly,' Sophie returned breathlessly. She *needed* to talk to him. She knew that it wasn't going to be a comfortable conversation, but talking couldn't have been further from her mind as he dragged at the waistband of her jeans, fumbling to undo the button and pull down the zipper.

She rested her hands on his broad shoulders and her mind went completely blank, swamped by the powerful churn of sensation. Her tee shirt was still over her breasts and she could feel the air cooling her heated nipples. She wanted him to lick them, suckle at them, but, like him, she was frantic for them to unite, to feel him moving in her, free and unencumbered, because she was now on the pill, so there was no need for him to reach for protection.

She helped with the jeans, tugging them down and then somehow wriggling out of them, while he, likewise, dealt with his trousers and boxers.

When she opened drugged eyes, she saw that his white shirt was unbuttoned all the way down, revealing a broad slither of bronzed chest, and he had dispensed with his shoes and socks. When had that happened? Her socks were tangled up with her trousers.

They'd barely closed the front door and here they were, practically naked in the hall, unable to keep their hands off one another.

Hands balled tightly behind her back, she literally couldn't keep still as he crouched in front of her and began tasting her, savouring her. She planted her legs apart to accommodate his questing mouth, barely able to breathe. When she glanced down to see his dark head moving between her legs, she felt unspeakably turned on.

'You need to come in me *now*!'

She heard his low laugh and then he was lifting her up and she was wrapping her legs around him, clinging to him as he began thrusting hard inside her, his hands supporting her bottom, her breasts bouncing as they moved together.

It was fast, furious, *raw* and earth-shattering. And utterly draining. For a short while, Sophie was transported to another place, another dimension, one in which difficult, awkward conversations with unpredictable outcomes didn't have to take place.

But as soon as she was back on her feet, hurriedly snatching clothes to put them on, her mind returned to what it had been chewing over before and she edged away from him, horrified at how easily she had dumped all her worries the second he had touched her.

And that was the essence of the problem, wasn't it? He did things to her, turned her to putty in his hands. He put her in a position where she couldn't seem to say *no* to him, which meant that this could go on until he got bored, and then he would chuck her aside and move on and where would her precious dignity be when that happened?

She was so cautious about never revealing the depth of her feelings for him, so fearful that he might gaze back into the past, understand how much she had meant to him then and work out how much he meant to her now. She was just so damned careful to play the adult game of keeping it cool, matching his control with control of her own.

She'd still be a mess when he decided that it was time to move on and he'd spot that in an instant.

The mere fact that she was about to tell him about that picture said it all but she didn't care because she had to find out.

'There's something I want to show you,' she told him in a rush, having put some vital distance between them. 'Well, something I want to ask you.' She sighed on a deep breath. 'Javier, we need to talk…'

CHAPTER TEN

'WHAT ABOUT?' HE TOOK his time getting dressed while she watched him from the door, arms folded, her expression revealing nothing. 'There's nothing more guaranteed to kill a good mood than *a talk*.'

'Are you speaking from personal experience?' Sophie asked coolly. She held up one interrupting hand even though he hadn't said anything. 'Of course you are. I suppose some of those women you went out with might have wanted a bit more from you than sex on tap.'

'Is that what this talk of yours is going to be about?' Javier's voice was as cool as hers, his expression suddenly wary and guarded.

Sophie spun round and began walking towards the kitchen. She could feel stinging colour washing over her because, in a way, this *was* about that. This *was* about more than just sex on tap.

'Well?' He caught up with her and held her arm, staying her, forcing her to turn to look at him. 'Is that what this *talk* of yours is going to be about? Wanting more?' He hadn't worked out the exact time scale, but it hit him that he had been seeing her now for several months, virtually on a daily basis, and he wasn't tiring of her. Immediately he felt his defences snap into position.

'I'm not an idiot,' Sophie lied valiantly. 'You'd have to be completely stupid to want *more* from a man like you!'

She yanked her arm free and glared at him. Her heart was thumping so hard and so fast in her chest that it felt as though it might explode.

She wanted to snatch the conversation back, stuff it away, take back wanting to *talk*. She wanted to pretend that she hadn't seen a picture of him at a gallery opening with some beautiful model clinging like a limpet to his arm, their body language saying all sorts of things she didn't want to hear.

'You're not capable of giving anyone anything more than sex,' she fumed, storming off towards the kitchen and the offending picture that she intended to fling in his face as proof of what she was saying.

'You weren't complaining five minutes ago,' he pointed out smoothly.

Below the belt, Sophie thought, but her face burnt when she thought about how her talk had taken a back seat the second he had touched her. He was right. She hadn't been complaining. In fact, at one point she remembered asking for more.

'I don't want more from you, Javier,' she gritted, reaching for the paper with shaking hands and flicking it open to the piece in the centre section. She tossed it to him and then stood at the opposite end of the table with her arms folded, nails biting into the soft flesh of her forearms. 'But what I *do* want is to know that you're not running around behind my back while we're an item!'

Javier stared down at the picture in front of him. He remembered the occasion distinctly. Another boring opening, this one at an art gallery. It had been full of just the sort of types he loathed—pretentious, champagne-drinking, caviar-scoffing crowds who had never given a penny to charity in their lives and had all attended top private schools courtesy of their wealthy parents. He could have given them a short lecture on the reality of being poor, but instead he had kept glancing at his watch and wondering what Sophie was doing.

As always, mixing in the jabbering, wealthy intel-lectual crowd was the usual assortment of beautiful hangers-on dressed in not very much and on the look-out for men with money. He had been a target from the very second he had walked through the door. He had shaken them off like flies, but by the end of the eve-ning he had more or less given up and that was when the photographer had obviously seen fit to take a com-promising snap.

In under a second, Javier could understand why So-phie had questions. He couldn't even remember the woman's name but he knew that she was a famous model and the way she was looking at him…the way she was holding on to his arm…

She didn't look like a woman on the verge of being cast aside by an indifferent stranger. Which she had been.

And snapped when, for five seconds, his attention had been caught by something the guy standing next to her had said to him and he was leaning into her, the very image of keen, while the guy to whom he had been speaking had been artfully cropped from the photo.

Not for a second was Javier tempted to launch into any kind of self-justifying speech. Why should he? He looked at her angry, hurt face and he ignored the thing inside him that twisted.

'Are you asking me to account for my actions when I'm not with you?'

'I don't think that's out of order on my part!'

'I have never felt the need to justify my behaviour to anyone. Ever.'

'Maybe you should have! Because when you're sleeping with someone, you are, actually, travelling down a two-way street whether you like it or not!'

'Meaning what?'

'Meaning it's not all about your world and what you want.'

'And maybe that will be the case one day, when I decide that I want more than a passing…situation with a woman.'

Sophie recoiled as though she had been physically struck. Suddenly all her anger seeped out of her and she was left feeling empty, hollow and utterly miserable.

Of course he would account for his behaviour one day. When he had met the right woman. In the meantime, he was having fun, and that was all that mattered. He wasn't tied to her any more than he had been tied to any of the women he had dated in the past, so if someone else came along and he was feeling energetic, then he probably thought, *why not?*

Facing up to that was like being kicked in the stomach. She literally reeled from the truth but she faced it anyway, just as she had faced the fact that she was still in love with him.

What was the point hiding from the truth? It didn't change anything. Having to deal with the mess her father had made of the company and the horror of her doomed marriage had taught her that, if nothing else.

'Did you sleep with that woman?'

'I'm not going to answer that question, Sophie.' Javier was incensed that, picture or no picture, she dared question his integrity. Did she think that he was the sort of man who couldn't control his libido and took sex wherever he found it?

He was also annoyed with himself for the way he had drifted along with this to the point where she felt okay about calling him to account. He'd been lazy. This had never been supposed to end up as anything more than an inconvenient itch that needed scratching. This had only ever been about finishing unfinished business.

'And maybe,' he said carefully, 'it's time for us to reassess what's going on here.'

Sophie nodded curtly. The ground had just fallen away from under her feet, but she wasn't going to plead or beg or hurl herself at him, because they really *did* need to 'reassess', as he put it.

'Your company is pretty much back on its feet.' He gave an expansive gesture while she waited in hopeless resignation for the Dear John speech he would soon be delivering.

She was too miserable to think about getting in there

first, being the first to initiate the break-up. It didn't matter anyway. The result was going to be the same.

'Your brother's disappeared back across the Atlantic and there's no need for you to continue taking an active part in the running of the company. The right people are all now in the right places to guide the ship. You can do whatever you want to do now, Sophie. Go back to university…get another job…disappear across the Atlantic to join your brother…'

Sophie's heart constricted because that was as good as telling her what he thought of her and she could have kicked herself for having been lulled into imagining that there was ever anything more to what they had.

'Or France.'

'Come again?'

'I've been thinking about it for a couple of weeks.'

Javier was at a loss as to what she was talking about. 'Thinking about…what, exactly?'

'Ollie's job is still up for grabs,' she said, thinking on her feet. 'And it's dealing with marketing, which is something I've found I rather like and I'm pretty good at.'

'You've been thinking about going to France?'

Sophie straightened. Did he think that she wasn't good enough for the job? Or did he think that she was always going to hang around until he got fed up with her, without giving any thought at all to life beyond Javier?

'Pretty much decided in favour of it,' she declared firmly. 'The house has found a buyer, as you know, who's happy to take it on and complete the renovations

I've started, so there's literally nothing keeping me here. Aside, that is, from Mum. And I think she'd be overjoyed to come and visit Paris once a month. And, of course, I can easily get to Cornwall to see her.'

'So you're telling me that you've been concocting this scheme behind my back for weeks?'

'It's not *a scheme*, Javier.' The more she thought about it, the better it sounded. How else would she get over him if she didn't put as much distance as she possibly could between them? Affairs were in order here. Why not? Too much of her life had been taken up having other people make decisions on her behalf. 'I wasn't sure exactly when, but seeing that picture of you in the newspaper…'

'For God's sake!' He tried hard to temper his voice. 'What the hell does some half-baked picture in a sleazy tabloid have to do with anything?'

'It's made me realise that it's time for me to take the next step.'

'Next step? What next step?' Javier raked his fingers through his hair and wished she would settle on one topic and stick there. He felt as though the carpet had been yanked from under his feet and he didn't like the feeling. 'Of course you can't go to bloody France! It's a ludicrous idea!'

'You can do what you like with whoever you want to…er…do it with, Javier, but it's time for me to get back into the dating scene, meet someone I can share my life with.' She tried to visualise this mystery man and drew a blank. 'I feel like my youth has been on hold and now I have a great opportunity to reclaim it.'

'In France?' He laughed scornfully.

'That's right.'

'And what if you'd never seen that picture?' He stopped just short of doing the unthinkable and telling her that he'd never met that woman in his life before and had no intention of ever meeting her again. Because his head was too wrapped up with *her*.

Unthinkable!

'It was just a question of time,' Sophie said truthfully. 'And that time's come.'

'You're telling me, after the sex we've just had, that you want out…' He laughed in disbelief and Sophie wanted to smack him because it was just the sort of arrogant reaction she might have expected.

'I'm telling you that the time has come when it has to be more than just the sex. So I'm going to find my soulmate,' she added quickly.

'You're going to find your *soulmate*?' Javier hated himself for prolonging this conversation. As soon as she had started kicking up a fuss about that picture, he should have told her that it was over. He didn't need anyone thinking that they had claim to him. Never had, never would, whatever he had told her about a woman coming along who could tame him. Wasn't going to happen.

Except… *She hadn't been trying to claim him, had she?*

She'd just reasonably asked him if there was anything going on with the airhead who had been dripping off his arm at a forgettable gallery opening and, instead of laughing and dismissing the idea, he had returned to his comfort zone, dug his heels in and stubbornly refused to answer.

And it was too late now to do anything about that.

Not that it would have made any difference, considering she had been making all sorts of plans behind his back.

For the best, he decided. So he'd become lazy but in truth the itch had been scratched a long time ago.

'Fine.' He held up both hands and laughed indulgently. 'Good luck with that one, Sophie. Experience has taught me that there's no such thing. I'm surprised given your past that you haven't had the same learning curve.'

'Just the opposite.' She felt nauseous as she watched him start heading for the door. 'Life's taught me that there are rainbows around every corner.'

'How...kitsch.' He saluted her and she remained where she was as he strode out of the kitchen.

And out of her life for good.

From Spain to France.

When you thought about it, it was a hop and a skip and it made perfect sense. He had had no input in Sophie's company for over three months. He had delegated responsibility to his trusted CEO and withdrawn from the scene.

He'd done his bit. He'd taken over, done what taking apart had needed doing and had put back together what had needed putting back together. The company was actually beginning to pull itself out of the quagmire of debt it had been languishing in for the past decade, and it was doing so in record time.

It was a success story.

He'd moved on and was focused on another takeover, this time a chain of failing hotels in Asia.

He was adding to his portfolio and, furthermore, branching out into new terrain, which was invigorating. By definition, branching out into anything new on the business front was going to be invigorating!

He had also just had a good holiday with his parents and had persuaded them to let him buy them a little place on the beach in the south of France, where they could go whenever they wanted to relax. He had pulled the trump card of promising that he would join them at least three times a year there and he had meant it.

Somehow, he had learnt the value of relaxation.

So what if he hadn't been able to relax in the company of any woman since he had walked out of Sophie's life?

He'd been bloody busy, what with his latest takeover and various company expansions across Europe.

But he was in Spain.

France seemed ridiculously close…

And he really ought to check, first hand, on the progress being made in the Parisian arm of a company which, all told, he part-owned…

And, if he *was* going to go to Paris, it made sense to drop in and see what Sophie was up to.

He knew that she had been working there for the past six weeks. It was his duty, after all, to keep tabs on the company. Everything was easily accessible on the computer, from the salary she was pulling in to where she lived and the apartment she was renting near Montmartre.

He was surprised that she hadn't headed off to more fulfilling horizons, leaving the running of the company to the experts, as her brother had.

His decision was made in moments. Already heading away from the first-class desk, he walked briskly back, ignoring the simpering blushes of the young girl who had just seen him.

A ticket to Paris. Next flight. First class.

Sophie let herself into her apartment, slamming the door against the fierce cold outside.

She was dressed in several layers but, even so, the biting wind still managed to find all sorts of gaps in those layers, working their way past them and finding the soft warmth of her skin.

Her face tingled as she yanked off the woolly hat, the scarf and the gloves, walking through her studio apartment and luxuriating in the warmth.

She had been incredibly lucky to have found the apartment that she had. It was small but cosy, comfortable and conveniently located.

And Paris was, as she had expected, as beautiful as she remembered it from the last time she had been there nearly ten years ago.

She had wanted to leave her comfort zone behind and she had! She had climbed out of her box and was now living in one of the most strikingly beautiful cities on the planet. Her mother had already been to visit her once and was determined to come again just as soon as the weather improved.

All in all, there were loads of girls her age who would have given their right arm to be where she was now!

And if she happened to be spending a Friday night in, with plans to curl up with her tablet in her flannel pyjamas and bedroom socks, then it was simply because it was just so cold!

When spring came, she would be out there, jumping right into that dating scene, as she had promised herself she would do before she had left England.

For the moment, she was perfectly happy just chilling.

And expecting no one to come calling because, although she had been out a few times with some of the other employees in the small arm of the company in Paris, she had not thus far met anyone who might just drop by on a Friday evening to see what she was up to.

That would come in time.

Probably in spring.

So when the doorbell went, she didn't budge. She just assumed it was someone selling something and she wasn't interested.

She gritted her teeth as the buzzer kept sounding and eventually abandoned all pretence of Zen calm as she stormed to the door and pulled it open, ready to give her uninvited caller a piece of her mind.

Javier had kept his finger on the buzzer. She was in. She had a basement apartment and he could see lights on behind the drawn curtains. He wondered whether she knew that basement apartments were at the highest risk of being burgled.

Since leaving Spain, he hadn't once questioned his decision to spring this visit on her, but now that he was here, now that he could hear the soft pad of footsteps, he felt his stomach clench with an uncustomary attack of nerves.

He straightened as she opened the door and for a few seconds something bewildering seemed to happen to him: he lost the ability to think.

'You're here…' he said inanely. Her long hair was swept over one narrow shoulder and she was wearing thick flannel bottoms and a long-sleeved thermal vest. And no bra. 'Do you always just open your door to strangers?' he continued gruffly, barely knowing where this unimaginative line of conversation was coming from.

'Javier!' Temporarily deprived of speech, Sophie could just blink at him, owl-like.

She'd pretended that she'd moved on. She was in Paris, she was enjoying her job, meeting new people…

How could she *not* have moved on? Hadn't that been the whole point of Paris?

But seeing him here, lounging against the door frame in a pair of faded black jeans and a black jumper, with his coat slung over his shoulder…

She was still in the same place she'd been when she'd watched him stroll out of her flat without a backwards glance.

How dared he just show up like this and scupper all her chances of moving on?

'What are you doing here? And how the heck did you find out where I live!'

'Computers are wonderful things. You'd be shocked at the amount of information they can divulge. Especially considering you work for a company I part-own...' Javier planted himself solidly in front of her. He hadn't given much thought to what sort of welcome he was likely to receive but a hostile one hadn't really crossed his mind.

Since when were women hostile towards him?

But since when was she just *any woman*?

She never had been and she never would be and, just like that, he suddenly felt sick. Sick and vulnerable in a way he had never felt before. Every signpost that had ever guided him, every tenet he had ever held dear, disappeared and he was left groping in the dark, feeling his way towards a realisation that had always been there at the back of his mind.

'Go away. I don't want to see you.'

Javier placed his hand on the door, preventing her from shutting it in his face. 'I've come...'

'For what?' Sophie mocked.

'I...'

Sophie opened her mouth and shut it because she didn't know what was going on. He looked unsettled. Confused. *Unsure.* Since when had Javier *ever* looked unsure?

'Are you all right?' she asked waspishly, relenting just enough to let him slip inside the apartment, but then shutting the door and leaning against it with her hands behind her back.

'No,' Javier said abruptly, looking away and then staring at her.

'What are you saying?' Sophie blanched. 'Are you...? *Are you ill...?*' Fear and panic gripped her in equal measure.

'Can we go sit somewhere?'

'Tell me what's wrong!' She was at his side in seconds, her small hand on his forearm, her eyes pleading for reassurance that he was okay because, whatever he was, he wasn't himself and that was scaring her half to death.

And if he saw that, she didn't care.

'I've missed you.' The words slipped out before Javier could stop them in their tracks. He had put everything on the line and he felt sick. He wondered why he hadn't thought to down a bottle of whisky before embarking on this trip.

'You've missed me?' Sophie squeaked.

'You asked what was wrong with me,' Javier threw at her accusingly.

'Is missing me wrong?' Something inside her burst and she wanted to laugh and cry at the same time. She had to tell herself that no mention had been made of love, and if he was missing her, then chances were that he was missing her body. Which was something else entirely.

She walked on wooden legs into the sitting room, where she had been watching telly on her tablet, and watched as he sat down, briefly glancing around him before settling those dark, dark eyes on her.

'Missing...' he sat down, arms loosely resting on his

thighs, his body leaning towards hers '…isn't something I've ever done.'

'Then it's a good thing,'

'I couldn't focus,' he admitted heavily. Now that he had started down this road, he had no alternative but to continue, although she hadn't chucked him out and that was a good thing. 'I couldn't sleep. You got into my head and I couldn't get you out of it.'

Sophie's heart was singing. She didn't want to speak. What if she broke the spell?

'I wanted you, you know…' He looked at her gravely. 'I don't think I ever really stopped wanting you, and when your brother showed up at my office, I figured I'd been handed the perfect way of putting that want to bed for good. Literally. I was going to just…go down the simple "exchange for favours" road. Cash for a little fun between the sheets, but then I decided that I wanted more than that… I didn't want a reluctant lover motivated for the wrong reasons.'

'You're assuming I would have given you your fun between the sheets because I needed money!' But she couldn't fire herself up to anger because her heart was still singing. She itched to touch him but first she wanted to talk.

'I'm arrogant.' He shot her a crooked smile. 'As you've told me a million times. I thought that it would be a one-night stand, simple as that, and then when you told me that you were a virgin…that the ex was gay…'

'Um, about that…'

'Sleeping with you that first time was…mind-blowing.'

'Er…'

'And it wasn't just because I'd never slept with a virgin before. It was because that person was *you*…'

'I should tell you something.' Sophie took a deep breath and looked him squarely in the eyes. So what if he hadn't said anything about love? He had opened up and she could tell from the way he was groping with his words that this was a first for him. A big deal. Her turn. It would be a bigger deal, but so be it.

'He wasn't gay. Roger wasn't gay. The opposite. He was one hundred percent straight as an arrow.'

Javier stared at her, for once in his life lost for words. 'You said…'

'No, Javier, *you* said.' She sighed wearily and sifted her fingers through her hair. 'It's such a long story and I'm sorry if I just let you think that Roger…'

Javier just continued staring, his agile brain trying and failing to make connections. 'Tell me from the beginning,' he said slowly.

'And you won't interrupt?'

'I promise nothing.'

Sophie half-smiled because why would this proud, stubborn, utterly adorable man ever take orders from anyone, even if it happened to be a very simple order?

'Okay…' Javier half-smiled back and a warm feeling spread through her 'I as good as half promise.'

'I'd been sort of going out with Roger by the time I went to university,' Sophie began, staring back into the past and not flinching away from it as she always did. 'I honestly don't know why except he'd been around for ever and it was something I just drifted into. It was cosy. We mixed in the same circles, had the same friends. His mother died when he was little and he and his father spent a good deal of time at our place. When his father died, he became more or less a fixture. He was crazy about me...' she said that without a trace of vanity '...and I think both my parents just assumed that we would end up getting married. Then I left home to go to university and everything just imploded.'

'Tell me,' Javier urged, leaning forward.

'Roger didn't want me to go to university. He was three years older and hadn't gone. He'd done an apprenticeship and gone straight into work at a local company. His parents had been very well off and he'd inherited everything as an only child, so there was no need for him to do anything high-powered and, in truth, he wasn't all that bright.'

She sighed. 'He wanted to have fun and have a wife to cater to him. But as soon as I went to university it hit me that I didn't love him. I liked him well enough but not enough to ever, ever consider marrying. I told him that but he wasn't happy and then I met you and... I stopped caring whether he was happy or not. I stopped caring about anyone or anything but you.'

'And yet you ended up marrying him. Doesn't make sense.'

'You promised you wouldn't interrupt.'

Javier raised both his hands in agreement. In truth, he was too intrigued by this tale to ask too many questions.

'My father summoned me back home,' she said. 'I went immediately. I knew it had to be important and I was worried that it was Mum. Her health hadn't been good and we were all worried for her. I never expected to be told that the family was facing bankruptcy.' She took a deep breath, eyes clouded. 'Suddenly it was like every bad thing that could happen at once had happened. Not only was the company on the verge of collapse but my father admitted that he had been ill— cancer—and it was terminal. Roger was presented to me as the only solution, given the circumstances.'

'Why didn't you come to me?'

'I wanted to but it was hard enough just fighting your corner without presenting you to my parents. They wanted nothing to do with you. They said that Roger would bring much-needed money to the table, money that would revitalise the company and drag it out of the red. Dad was worried sick that he wouldn't be around long enough to do anything about saving the company. He was broken with guilt that he had allowed things to go down the pan but I think his own personal worries, which he had kept to himself, must have been enormous.

'They told me that what I felt for you was…infatuation. That I was young and bowled over by someone who would be no good for me in the long run. You weren't in my social class and you were a foreigner. Those two things would have been enough to condemn you but, had it not been for what was happening in the company, I don't think they would have dreamt of forcing my hand.'

'But they persuaded you that marrying Roger was vital to keep the family business afloat,' Javier recapped slowly. 'And, with your father facing death, there wasn't time for long debates…'

'I still wouldn't have,' Sophie whispered. 'I was so

head over heels in love with you, and I told Roger that. Pleaded with him to see it from my point of view. I knew that if he backed me up, Mum and Dad might lay off the whole convenient marriage thing, but of course he didn't back me up. He was red with anger and jealousy. He stormed off. At the time, he had a little red sports car...'

'He crashed, didn't he?'

Sophie nodded and Javier picked up the story.

'And you felt...guilty.'

'Yes. I did. Especially because it was a very bad accident. Roger was in hospital for nearly two months and, by the time he was ready to come out, I had resigned myself to doing what had to be done. I'd even come to half believe that perhaps Mum and Dad were right—perhaps what I felt for you was a flash in the pan, whereas my relationship with Roger had the weight of shared history, which would prove a lot more powerful in the long run.'

Javier was seeing what life must have been like for her. In a matter of a few disastrous weeks, her entire future and a lot of her past had been changed for ever. She hadn't used him. He had simply been a casualty of events that had been far too powerful for her to do anything about but bow her head and follow the path she had been instructed to follow.

Not old enough to know her own mind, and too attached to her parents to rebel, she had simply obeyed them.

'But it didn't go according to plan...' he encouraged.

'How did you guess? It was a disaster from the very

start. We married but the accident had changed Roger.
Maybe, like me, he went into it thinking that we could
give it a shot, but there was too much water under the
bridge. And there had been after-effects from the accident. He very quickly became addicted to painkillers.
He used to play a lot of football but he no longer could.
Our marriage became a battleground. He blamed me,
and the more he blamed me, the guiltier I felt. He had
affairs, which he proudly told me about. He wreaked
havoc with the company. He gambled. There was nothing I could do because he could quickly turn violent. By
the time he died, I'd…I'd grown up for ever.'

Javier looked at her long and hard. 'Why did you let
me believe that he was gay?'

'Because…' She took a deep breath. 'I thought that if
you knew the whole story, you would know how much
you meant to me then and you would quickly work out
how much you mean to me now.' She laughed sadly.
'And, besides that, I've always felt ashamed—ashamed
that I let myself be persuaded into doing something I
really didn't want to do.'

'When you say that I *mean something to you now…*'

'I know what this is for you, Javier. You believed that
I ran out on you, and when you had the chance, you
figured you would take what should have been yours
all those years ago.'

Javier had the grace to flush. What else could he do?

'And, for a while, I kidded myself that that was what
it was for me too. I'd dreamt about you for seven years
and I'd been given the chance to turn those dreams into

reality, except for me it was much more than that. You won't want to hear this but I'll tell you anyway. I never stopped loving you. You were the real thing, Javier. You'll always be the main event in my life.'

'Sophie…' He closed the distance between them but only so that he could sit closer to her, close enough to thread his fingers through hers. His throat ached. 'I've missed you so much. I thought I could walk away, just like I thought that sleeping with you would be a simple solution to sorting out the problem of you being on my mind all the time through the years. There, at the back of my mind like a ghost that refused to go away. You'd dumped me and married someone else. It didn't matter how many times I told myself that I was well rid of someone who used me for a bit of fun until she got her head together and realised that the person she really wanted to be with wasn't me… I still couldn't forget you.'

Sophie thought that this was one of those conversations she never wanted to end. She just wanted to keep repeating it on a loop, over and over and over.

'We slept together, Sophie, and just like that my life changed. Not having you in it was unthinkable. I didn't even register that consciously until you presented me with that picture and I suddenly realised that I had succumbed to all the things I'd thought I'd ruled out of my life. You'd domesticated me to the point where I didn't want to be anywhere unless you were there, and I hadn't even realised it. I took fright, Soph. I suddenly felt the walls closing in and I reacted on instinct and scarpered.'

'And now that you're back…' She had to say this. 'I can't have a relationship with you, Javier. I can't go back to living from one day to the next, not knowing whether you'll decide that you're bored and that you have to take off.'

'How could I ever get bored with you, Sophie?' He lightly touched her cheek with his fingers and realised that he was trembling. 'And how can you not see what I need to tell you? I don't just want you, but I need you. I can't live without you, Sophie. I fell in love with you all those years ago and, yes, you're the main event in my life as well and always will be. Why do you think I came here? I came because *I had to*. I just couldn't stand not being with you any longer.'

Sophie flung herself at him and he caught her in his arms, laughing because the chair very nearly toppled over.

'So, will you marry me?' he whispered into her hair and she pulled back, smiling, wanting to laugh and shout all at the same time.

'You mean it?'

'With every drop of blood that flows through my veins. Let me show you how great marriage can be.' He laughed. 'I never thought I'd hear myself say that.'

'Nor did I.' She kissed him softly and drew back. 'And now that you have, I won't allow you to take it back, so, yes, my darling. I'll marry you…'

* * * * *

Turn the page for an exclusive extract of
SLEEPLESS IN MANHATTAN,
the first book in USA TODAY *bestselling author*
Sarah Morgan's enthralling new trilogy,
FROM MANHATTAN WITH LOVE*!*

PAIGE STOOD FOR a moment, thinking how unpredictable life was.

Who would have thought that herself, Eva and Frankie losing their jobs would have turned out so well?

Urban Genie existed only because life had laid a twist in her path.

Change had been forced on her, but it had proved to be a good thing.

Instead of fighting it, she should embrace it.

What had Jake said?

Sometimes you have to let life happen.

Maybe she should try to do that a bit more.

And maybe one day she'd look back and realize that *not* being with Jake was the best thing that could have happened—because if she'd been with Jake she wouldn't have met—

Who?

Would she ever meet someone who made her feel the way Jake did?

She stood leaning on the railing, gazing at the city she loved.

The lights of Manhattan sparkled like a thousand stars against a midnight sky and now, finally, as the last of the guests made their way to the elevators, she allowed herself a moment to enjoy it.

"Time to relax and celebrate, I think."

Jake's voice came from behind her and she turned to find him holding two glasses of champagne. He handed her one. "To Urban Genie."

"I don't drink while I'm working." And while Jake was present this was definitely still work.

She knew better than to lower her guard a second time.

"The guests have gone. You're no longer working. Your job is done."

"I'm not off duty until the clear-up has finished." And then tomorrow would be the follow-up, the post-mortem. Discussions on what they might have done differently. They'd unpick every part of the event and put it back together again. By the time they'd finished they'd have found every weak spot and strengthened it.

"I don't think one glass of champagne is going to impair your ability to supervise that. Congratulations." He tapped his glass against hers. "Spectacular. Any new business leads?"

"Plenty. First up is a baby shower next week. Not much time to prepare, but it's a good event."

He winced. "A baby shower is *good*?"

"Yes. Partly because the woman throwing it for her pregnant colleague is CEO of a fashion importer. But all business is good."

"Chase Adams is impressed. By tomorrow word will

have got around that Urban Genie is the best event concierge company in Manhattan. Prepare to be busy."

"I'm prepared."

His praise warmed her. Her heart lifted.

He stood next to her and the brush of his sleeve against her bare arm made her shiver.

His gaze collided briefly with hers and she thought she saw a blaze of heat, but then he looked away and she did, too, her face burning.

She was doing it again. Imagining things.

And it had to stop.

It had to stop right now.

No more embarrassing herself. No more embarrassing *him*.

She turned her head to look at him but he was staring straight ahead, his handsome face blank of expression.

"Thank you," she said.

"For what?"

"For asking us to do this. For giving us free rein and no budget. For trusting us. For inviting influential people and decision-makers. For making Urban Genie happen." She realized how much she owed him. "I hate accepting help—"

"I know, but that isn't what happened here. You did it yourself, Paige."

"But I wouldn't have been able to do it without you. I'm grateful. If you hadn't suggested it, pushed me that night on the terrace, I wouldn't have done it." She breathed in. Now was as good a time as any to say everything that needed to be said. And if she said it aloud, maybe it would help both of them. "There's

something else—" She saw him tense and felt a flash
of guilt that he felt the need to be defensive around her.
Definitely time to clear the air. "I owe you an apology."

"For what?"

"For misreading the situation the other night. For
making things awkward between us. I was…" She hesi-
tated, trying to find the right words. "I guess you could
say I was doing an Eva. I was looking for things that
weren't there. I was close to panic and you were trying
to distract me. I understand that now. I don't want you
feeling that you have to avoid me, or be careful around
me. I'd never want that. I—"

"Don't. Don't apologize."

He gripped the railing and she noticed his knuck-
les were white.

"I wanted to clear it up, that's all. It was a kiss. Didn't
mean anything. Two people trapped in an elevator, one
of whom was feeling vulnerable." *Shut up right now,
Paige.* "I know I'm not your type. I know you don't
have those feelings. I'm like your little sister. I get that.
So—"

"Oh, for— *Seriously?*" He interrupted her with a
low growl and finally turned to face her. "After what
happened the other night you really think I see you as
a little sister? You think I could kiss you that way if I
felt like that about you?"

She stared at him, her heart drumming a rhythm
against her chest. "I thought— You said— I thought
you saw me that way."

"Yeah, well, I tried." He gave a humorless laugh and
drained his champagne in one mouthful. "God knows,

I tried. I've done everything short of asking Matt for a baby photo of you and sticking that to my wall. Nothing works. And do you know why? Because I *do* have feelings, you're *not* little and you're not my damn *sister*."

Shock struck her like a bolt of lightning.

They were the only two people left on the terrace. Just them and the Manhattan night. The buildings rose around them—dark shapes enveloping them in intimate shadows and the shimmer of light.

The storm clouds were gathering, creating ominous shadows in the dark sky.

The sudden lick of wind held the promise of rain.

Paige was oblivious. The sky might have come crashing down and she wouldn't have noticed.

Her mouth was so dry she could hardly form the words. "But if you feel that way, if you do have feelings, why do you keep saying—" She stumbled over the words, confused. "Why haven't you ever done anything about it?"

"Why do you think?"

There was a cynical, bitter edge to Jake's tone that didn't fit the nature of their conversation. None of the pieces fitted. She couldn't think. Everything about her had ceased to function.

"Because of Matt?"

"Partly. He'd kick my butt. And I wouldn't blame him." He stared down at his hands, as if they were something that didn't belong to him. As if he was worried about what they might do.

"Because you're not interested in relationships—or 'complications' as you call them?"

"Exactly."

"But sex doesn't have to be a relationship. It can just be sex. You said so yourself."

"Not with you."

His tone was harsh and she took a step back, shocked. They'd often argued, baited each other, but she'd never heard that edge of steel in his voice before.

"Why? What's different about me?"

"I'm not going to screw you and walk away, Paige. That's not going to happen."

"Because of our friendship? Because you're worried it would be awkward?"

"Yeah, that, too."

"Too? What else?" She stared at him, bemused.

He was silent.

"Jake? What else?"

He swore under his breath. "Because I care about you. I don't want to hurt you. There's already been enough damage to your heart. You don't need more."

The first raindrops started to fall.

Paige was still oblivious.

Her head spun with questions. *Where? What? Why? How much?* "So you— Wait—" She struggled to make sense of it. "You're saying that you've been *protecting* me? No. That can't be true. You're the only one who *doesn't* protect me. When everyone else is wrapping me in cotton wool, you handle me as though you're throwing the first pitch at a game."

He didn't protect her. He *didn't*. Not Jake.

She waited for him to agree with her, to confirm that he didn't protect her.

He was silent.

There was a throbbing in her head. She lifted her fingers to her forehead and rubbed. The storm was closing in—she could feel it. And not just in the sky above her.

"I *know* you don't protect me." She tried to focus, tried to examine the information and shook her head. "Just the other night, when we found out we'd lost our jobs, Matt was sympathetic but you were brutal. I was ready to cry, but you made me so *angry* and—" She stared at him, understanding. She felt the color drain from her face. "You did it on purpose. You made me angry on purpose."

"You get more done when you're angry," he said flatly. "And you needed to get things done."

No denial.

He'd goaded her. Galvanized her into action.

"You challenge every idea I have." She felt dizzy. "We fight. All the time. If I say something is black, you say it's white."

He stood in silence, not bothering to deny it, and she shook her head in disbelief.

"You *make* me angry. You do that on purpose. Because if I'm angry with you, then I'm not—" She'd been blind. She breathed hard, adjusting to this new picture of their relationship. The first boom of thunder split the air but she ignored it. "How long? How long, Jake?"

"How long, what?" He yanked at his bow tie with impatient fingers.

His gaze shifted from hers. He looked like a man who wanted to be anywhere but with her.

"How long have you cared? How long have you been

p-protecting me?" She stumbled over the word—and the thought.

He ran his hand over his jaw. "Since I walked through the door of that damn hospital room and saw you sitting on the bed in your Snoopy tee shirt, with that enormous smile on your face. You were so brave. The most frightened brave person I'd ever seen. And you tried so hard not to let anyone see it. I have *always* protected you, Paige. Except for the other night, when I let my guard down."

But he'd been protecting her then, too. He'd been taking care of her when she'd been so terrified she hadn't known what to do.

"So you thought I was brave, but not strong? Not strong enough to cope alone without protection? I don't understand. I thought you weren't interested, that you didn't want this, and now I discover—" It was a struggle to process it. "So this whole time you *did* care about me. You *do*."

Rain was falling steadily now, landing in droplets on his jacket and her hair.

"Paige—"

"The kiss the other night—"

"Was a mistake."

"But it was real. It wasn't because I was a pair of red lips in an elevator. All these days, months, *years* I've been telling myself you didn't feel anything. All the time I've been confused because my instincts were so wrong and I couldn't understand why. But now I do. They weren't wrong. *I* wasn't wrong."

"Maybe you weren't."

"So why let me think that?"

"Because it was easier."

"Easier than what? Telling me the truth? News flash—and, by the way, I thought you knew this—I don't want to be protected. I want to live my life. You're the one who's always telling me to take more risks."

"Yeah, well, that proves you shouldn't listen to anything I tell you. We should go inside before you catch pneumonia."

He eased away from the railings and she caught his arm.

"I'll go inside when I decide to go inside." The rain was soaking her skin. "What happens now?"

"Nothing. I know you don't want to be protected but that's tough, Paige, because that's what I'm doing. I'm not what you're looking for and I never have been. We don't want the same thing. There's a car waiting downstairs to take you and the other two home. Make sure you use it."

Without giving her a chance to respond, Jake strode away from her toward the bank of elevators and left her standing there, alone in the glittering cityscape, watching the entire shape of her life change. Another twist. Another turn. The unexpected.

Don't miss SLEEPLESS IN MANHATTAN
by Sarah Morgan, available from HQN Books.

#3453 MARRYING HER ROYAL ENEMY
Kingdoms & Crowns
by Jennifer Hayward

Most women would kill to be draped in ivory and walking up the aisle toward King Kostas Laskos. But Stella Constantinides naively bared her heart to Kostas to disastrous effect once before and this feisty princess refuses to be his pawn ever again.

#3454 HIS MISTRESS FOR A WEEK
by Melanie Milburne

Years ago, Clementine Scott clashed spectacularly with arrogant architect Alistair Hawthorne and swore she'd never have anything to do with him again! But when Clem's brother disappears with Alistair's stepsister, she's forced to go with Alastair to Monte Carlo to retrieve them!

#3455 IN THE SHEIKH'S SERVICE
by Susan Stephens

Sheikh Shazim Al Q'Aqabi must resist his instant attraction to mysterious dancer Isla Sinclair, for duty is Shazim's only mistress. Until Isla is revealed as the prize winner who will travel to the desert to work with him...making their chemistry impossible to ignore.

#3456 CLAIMING HIS WEDDING NIGHT
by Louise Fuller

Addie Farrell's marriage to casino magnate Malachi King lasted exactly one day, until she discovered their love was a sham. Now Addie must prepare to face her husband—and their dangerously seductive chemistry—once again!

YOU CAN FIND MORE INFORMATION ON UPCOMING HARLEQUIN® TITLES, FREE EXCERPTS AND MORE AT WWW.HARLEQUIN.COM.

HPCNM0716RB

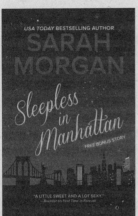

$7.99 U.S./$9.99 CAN.

EXCLUSIVE
Limited Time Offer

$1.⁰⁰ OFF

USA TODAY **Bestselling Author**

SARAH MORGAN

introduces From Manhattan with Love, *a sparkling new trilogy about three best friends embracing life—and love—in New York.*

Paige Walker loves a challenge, but can she convince a man who trusts no one to take a chance on forever?

Sleepless in Manhattan

Available May 31, 2016.
Pick up your copy today!

HQN

$1.⁰⁰ OFF the purchase price of SLEEPLESS IN MANHATTAN by Sarah Morgan.

Offer valid from May 31, 2016, to July 31, 2016. Redeemable at participating retail outlets. Not redeemable at Barnes & Noble. Limit one coupon per purchase. Valid in the U.S.A. and Canada only.

52613760

5 65373 00076 2   (8100)0 12167

"I came here to set a few things straight with you," Rahim
sneered, deeply resentful that she'd led him to question
himself when there was no doubt where his destiny lay.
"You thought what happened in Dar-Aman wouldn't go
unchallenged. You were wrong."

Allegra's hand jerked to her stomach, her eyes more
vivid against her ashen colour. "No. Please..."

From across the room, Rahim saw her sway. With a
curse, he charged forward and caught her as her legs gave
way. It occurred to him then that she hadn't answered him
when he'd asked what ailed her. Swinging her up into his
arms, he carried her to the sofa and laid her down.

With a low moan, she tried to get up. Rahim stayed her
with a firm hand. "I'm going to get you some water. Then
you'll tell me what's wrong with you. And what the hell
you're doing giving long speeches and photo ops when
you should be in bed."

Her mouth pursed mutinously for a moment before she gave a small nod.

Rising, he crossed to the bar and poured a glass of water. She'd sat up by the time he returned. Silently she took the water and sipped, her wary eyes following him as he sat on the sturdy coffee table directly in front of her.

"Now tell me what's wrong with you."

The sleek knot at her nape had come undone during the journey to the sofa, and twin falls of chocolate-brown hair framed her face as she bent her head. Rahim gritted his teeth against the urge to brush it back, soothe whatever was troubling her, reassure her that he meant her no harm.

He was so busy fighting his baser urges, and sternly reminding himself that he was in the right and she in the wrong, that he didn't hear her whispered words.

"What did you say?"

Her jerky inhale wobbled the glass in her hands. "I said I'm not sick, but I can't go to prison because I'm pregnant." She raised her head then and stared back at him with eyes black with despair. "I'm carrying your child, Rahim."

Don't miss
THE DI SIONE SECRET BABY
by Maya Blake,
available August 2016 wherever
Harlequin Presents® books and ebooks are sold.

www.Harlequin.com

JUST CAN'T GET ENOUGH
OF THE ALPHA MALE?
Us either!

Come join us at **I Heart Presents** to hear the latest from your favorite Harlequin Presents authors and get special behind-the-scenes secrets of the Presents team!

With access to the latest breaking news and special promotions, **I Heart Presents** is *the* destination for all things Presents. Get up close and personal with the sexy alpha heroes who make your heart beat faster and share your love of these glitzy, glamorous reads with the authors, the editors and fellow Presents fans!